PATRICK GRIFFIN'S
FIRST
BIRTHDAY ON ITH

Also by Ned Rust

Patrick Griffin's Last Breakfast on Earth

PATRICK GRIFFIN'S
FIRST
BIRTHDAY on ITH

NED RUST

Illustrations by
JAKE PARKER

ROARING BROOK PRESS
New York

Published by Roaring Brook Press
Roaring Brook Press is a division of Holtzbrinck Publishing Holdings
Limited Partnership
175 Fifth Avenue, New York, NY 10010

mackids.com

Library of Congress Cataloging-in-Publication Data

Names: Rust, Ned, author.
Title: Patrick Griffin's first birthday on Ith / Ned Rust
Description: First edition. | New York : Roaring Brook Press, 2017. |
    Series: Patrick Griffin and the three worlds ; book 2 | Summary:
    While twelve-year-old Patrick and his friend Oma, protected by a
    powerful griffin, work to overthrow Ith's sinister government,
    Mr. BunBun races to warn humans of impending doom on Earth.
Identifiers: LCCN 2016038472 (print) | LCCN 2017018042 (ebook) |
    ISBN 9781626723450 (ebook) | ISBN 9781626723443 (hardback)
Subjects: | CYAC: Fantasy. | Space and time—Fiction. | Heroes—
    Fiction. | BISAC: JUVENILE FICTION / Science Fiction. | JUVENILE
    FICTION / Action & Adventure / General. | JUVENILE FICTION /
    Humorous Stories.
Classification: LCC PZ7.1.R875 (ebook) | LCC PZ7.1.R875 Paf 2017
    (print) | DDC [Fic]—dc23
LC record available at https://lccn.loc.gov/2016038472

Our books may be purchased in bulk for promotional, educational, or
business use. Please contact your local bookseller or the Macmillan
Corporate and Premium Sales Department at (800) 221-7945 ext. 5442
or by e-mail at MacmillanSpecialMarkets@macmillan.com.

First edition 2017
Book design by Elizabeth H. Clark

Printed in the United States of America
by LSC Communications, Harrisonburg, Virginia

1 3 5 7 9 10 8 6 4 2

For Ruth

CONTENTS

PART I: POTENTATES

PART II: PRIMATES

PART III: PISMIRES

I believe in aristocracy, though—if that is the right word, and if a democrat may use it. Not an aristocracy of power, based upon rank and influence, but an aristocracy of the sensitive, the considerate and the plucky. Its members are to be found in all nations and classes, and all through the ages, and there is a secret understanding between them when they meet. They represent the true human tradition, the one permanent victory of our queer race over cruelty and chaos. Thousands of them perish in obscurity, a few are great names. They are sensitive for others as well as for themselves, they are considerate without being fussy, their pluck is not swankiness but the power to endure, and they can take a joke.

—E. M. FORSTER, *Two Cheers for Democracy*

PROLOGUE

HE'S BACK," SAID MY-CHALE.

"Who's back?" asked Oma, startling awake at the sound of the griffin's voice.

Patrick was already up, roused by a dream that in its own way had been far, far louder than My-Chale's words. "Rex," he said to Oma.

He and My-Chale looked at each other across the dimly lit room. They had just had the very same nightmare.

PART I: POTENTATES

Sticks and stones
will break the bones
of those whose words
have ever hurt us.

—bcp §308¶86 via Enureticus Balbus

CHAPTER 1
Hide, Rabbit, Hide

MR. BUNBUN HAD DEFEATED ONE AND FOOLED three, but surviving *five* of Rex's assassins was going to be tough. Especially running blind like this. Well, not literally blind—he had no trouble *seeing* the gray, rainy, swampy, garbage-strewn forest around him—but data-wise everything had gone dark. No more Wi-Fi, 3G, 4G, or LTE, and no more GPS. No more binky.

The device had come with him from Ith. It sometimes resembled a smartphone, but it folded open, folded smaller, could be placed over your eyes like a virtual reality visor, and could generate holographs. It was really, BunBun had to admit, a marvel of technology. You could spend your entire life without one and think you were happy and fine. But pick one up, and by the time you thought to put it down, it was too late. You were a full-blown addict—all panicky and insecure whenever you were deprived even for an afternoon!

His desperation was all the worse because the little device had saved his life *twice* in the few days since he'd arrived on Earth. And, given how this morning was going, he was going to need some lifesaving again very shortly.

But he'd had to give it up. He'd been very careful, kept a low profile, had only gone on the network when he'd absolutely had to. He'd kept his encryption protocols running the entire time and never accessed the grid from the same exact place or with the same service provider twice. But Rex's people had somehow identified his signal and were now coming for him.

And so, in a city called Yonkers, he'd activated the Red Herring app his friends on Ith had installed and had stuck the binky in the back of a cheesecake truck. The app would have it repeatedly do Internet searches for *Rex Abraham*, *deacons*, and *purge*, terms that would surely further draw the attention of his pursuers, as the truck made its deliveries.

The ploy might buy some time and distance, but it wouldn't be a permanent reprieve. His enemies were too resourceful and numerous, and he was too resourceless and alone.

And there were far too many cameras. Sooner or later he'd be spotted by a traffic or security cam, a smartphone, a surveillance vehicle or drone. And then, in a matter of moments, his image would be uploaded onto the network and identified and—*ping-click-bang*—his mission to make it to the center of New York City and save the Earth would come to a hasty end.

He had a sudden impulse to sit down and cry, but one of his favorite entries from *The Book of Commonplace*—the curated collection of practical and spiritual wisdom from across the three worlds—came to him.

He whispered the line aloud: " 'If you don't act like there's hope, there is no hope.' "

He chided himself. Yes, he was a stranger in an imperiled land, running toward a goal that might be impossible, running away from an organization of killers about to murder *billions* of people. But was he therefore supposed to give up? Was he supposed to sit on his furry tail and wait for something bad to happen? Or exert himself and have the same bad something happen anyway?

Another *Commonplace* line came to him then: "Heroes are ready to fail so as not to quit. Cowards are ready to quit so as not to fail." He whispered it aloud, too, then charged up the next hill, pumping his heavy, wet-furred arms and legs.

Through the forest's just-budding branches, he spotted a six-lane highway ahead and a footbridge off to the right. He paused and removed a burr clinging to his left shoulder. Then he aimed his antlered head at the bridge and bounded down the slope.

He didn't notice the two early-morning joggers till he was nearly upon them. The first screamed like she'd seen a rat, and the other, full of New York attitude and vocabulary, yelled, "What the @#$! is *that*!!?" as she reached for her smartphone.

BunBun raced past and dove into the woods on the far side of the bridge.

Praying she hadn't managed to snap his picture, he sprinted up the next wooded hill and soon reached its rocky, graffiti-splattered summit. He gasped as he took in the vista. Past the dew-covered baseball, soccer, Ultimate, and cricket fields of Van Cortlandt Park was the bristling, concrete-and-glass sprawl of one of the biggest cities ever built on *any* world.

The scale of it was almost too much to accept. There were some very tall towers on Ith, but they were few and far between, not piled up against each other like this. The other thing that struck him was how relatively shoddy and chaotic every-thing seemed. The buildings and vehicles of Ith were so crisp and sparkly. Here were jagged-looking chimneys, derelict water towers, crooked rooftop antennas, dangling wires, garbage cans overflowing with dirty plastic, trucks with spray-painted sides, cars with dented hoods and missing hubcaps—

"Oh no," he said, his eyes spotting a lime-green van. The logo on its side was a large hexagon-headed virus particle. Rainbow-colored letters above and beneath read, *KINGA-ROO Data Solutions: Rebooting the World in Broadband.*

A technology truck parked on a busy road in a busy city was of course not alarming in itself, but the virus symbol was exactly the same as the one on the flags and uniforms of Ith. It was Rex's standard.

The slogan, too, fairly stank of the Decimator of Worlds' touch. "The Reboot" was what he and his Deacons had called the destruction of Ith's population four decades ago. And doubtless it would be what Rex and his fascistic followers called the identical disaster they planned for Earth.

BunBun swiveled his big ears like radar dishes and, through the noise of the wakening city, made out purposeful footsteps crunching the dry, dead leaves. Another sound accompanied them—the muted but distinctive whining of a high-amperage portable electronic device.

Every hair on his body stood erect. This was bad.

He needed to find a place to hide, and quickly.

CHAPTER 2
Secret Understandings

ON THE MORNING OF PATRICK GRIFFIN'S THIRTEENTH birthday, all six of his siblings were gathered in the attic room of his oldest sister, Lucie. Them all gathering together without their parents had almost never happened before. Them doing so in Lucie's room had *definitely* never happened before.

Fourteen-year-old Neil was hunched over Lucie's laptop watching (not searching, which might attract the attention of the people they'd been warned about) for news regarding giant jackalopes or adults with two first names.

Sitting on Lucie's bed were Patrick's second-youngest sister, Carly, reading a yellow *Pretty Little Liars* paperback, and his second-oldest sister, Eva, browsing Snapchat stories on her cracked-screen iPhone.

Lucie herself stood by the window working at her sketchbook with a piece of charcoal, and the youngest—the four-year-old Twins—played with their plastic dinosaurs and mastodons by the closed closet door.

Although it was a Thursday, there would be no school or sports for any of them today. They were staying home as they had every day that week.

Probably next week they'd all go back to their regular routines. Life had to return to normal, regardless of whether Patrick came home. And they were fairly certain he wouldn't.

The Griffin children had a secret understanding of their brother's situation from Mr. BunBun, the big-antlered rabbit they had met on Monday.

The creature had come from another world, a world called Ith—the very same world where, he said, Patrick had just been sent.

It was all too crazy to believe. But when you hear something like this from a giant talking jackalope with a futuristic, holograph-projecting smartphone, somehow the insanity of it seems less than completely insane.

His device—a "binky," he called it—had played them mind-blowing images and videos of this other world. It was a world inhabited by people whose eyes were too big and ears too small, who wore lots of makeup (even men and children), who wore foot-gloves rather than regular shoes, and who lived in windowless houses with sheep and goats on their grass-covered roofs.

There were pristine forests, sky-cars, stratosphere-touching sky-scrapers, flying drones, and six-wheeled delivery robots.

BunBun had then showed them grainy pictures of bombed-out cities, work-slaves wearing blue collars, and scary figures in hooded robes called Deacons who were the surgically enhanced rulers of the world and were all known by two first names—Sabrina Kim, Helen Kelly, Matthew Roy, and so on.

Finally, there were photos, videos, and holographs of the world's exalted leader, Rex Abraham.

The man's close-set eyes, pouty lips, and dimpled chin reminded Eva of Dr. Schoen, the Griffin family orthodontist. Neil agreed that might be so but pointed out that, from the neck down, his muscular build more resembled that of J. J. Watt, the famous football player. (Dr. Schoen had skinny arms and a belly that pressed in on your shoulder when he checked your braces.) They all agreed, at any rate, that this Rex was a seriously scary-looking individual.

The big jackalope then went on to tell them that Ith had once been just like Earth but Rex and his two-first-name accomplices had taken over and killed everybody over the age of three. Over the following decades, Rex and his people had rebuilt this other world into the tightly controlled, high-tech surveillance state that it was today.

But if Ith was more technologically advanced than Earth, it was also more fantastical. Last of all, BunBun showed them pictures of monsters and creatures even more strange than his jackalope self—giants, dragons, talking balls of light, unicorns, sea monsters—and told them these creatures still lived on Ith, and that they once had on Earth, too.

"So you're saying," Lucie had said, "the reason we have legends and stories about dragons and ogres and stuff is that there actually used to be some of them here on Earth?"

"It's hard to say," the rabbit had replied, "because Rex has already so doctored your world's history, but yes, I believe there *used* to be quite a lot of us here. And there may in fact be a few of us left. Obviously ones who are very good at hiding."

CHAPTER 3
Travel Light, Travel at Night

THEY TRAVELED AFTER THE SUN WENT DOWN; THEY
traveled by air; they traveled west. They traveled toward
a destination they hoped would be among the last places the
Deacons would look for them; they traveled with a nagging
fear it might be the first.

Oma and Patrick, riding on the back of My-Chale, the
griffin, the leader of the Commonplacers, were headed to the
ruins of a northwestern American city called Seattle, another
location the Deacons were still in the slow, methodical process of dismantling, erasing from the face of the planet.

My-Chale said there was somebody important they needed
to meet there. Somebody named Ivan Dunn.

All Patrick knew was that he hoped it would be warmer in Seattle than it was here over the scrubby hills of what had once been the state of Wyoming.

My-Chale, being a griffin, had fur and feathers to ward off the cold. Patrick and Oma, meanwhile, only had their way-too-thin camouflage bodysuits and a tattered, grease-stained tarp they were using as a blanket. They'd found it in the back of an abandoned garage they'd stopped in earlier that night. It smelled of motor oil, mildew, and something much worse.

Another wave of goose bumps migrated up Patrick's arms as he stared off into the night.

Below, barely visible in the light of the just-risen moon, the rusting hulk of an old-fashioned tanker truck had trapped tumbleweeds the way a tide-stranded log at the beach gathers seaweed.

It had been more than four decades since anybody had lived out here.

A yellow-orange glow flared in the northern sky.

"What was that?" Patrick turned and asked Oma.

But she was asleep.

"A collar camp, most likely," said My-Chale, craning his enormous eagle head back over his shoulder. He'd done this before, and it made Patrick nervous. Like when his grandmother turned around to talk while she was driving.

"Oh," said Patrick. Collar camps were where they sent "belties," prisoners of the government. The Deacons placed people they didn't like in body-controlling collars, just as they did with service animals. There were no power lawn mowers or hedge trimmers on Ith. Remote-controlled goats, sheep, cows, llamas, and even squirrels kept their gardens, yards, and arboretums neat.

Collared humans didn't do yard work, however. The Deacons sent them off on secret details. The regular people of Ith knew about them—among the unkind children of Ith, the term *belty* was employed much as *loser* was on Earth—but, like prisoners in most societies, they were kept away from the regular citizenry.

"Out here it's probably a mining operation," continued the griffin. "Or maybe even a former military site. Those tend to be high-value reclamation targets."

More than forty years after the pandemic that had decimated Ith's population, the Deacons were still dismantling and recycling the massive remains of the former world. Patrick had seen them taking down the abandoned husk of Ith's version of New York City just two days ago.

"Are these the Rockies?" asked Patrick, eyeing the moonlit snow on a peak maybe twenty miles ahead. They seemed to have finally made it across the bleak western plains.

"Ah, yes," said My-Chale, banking sharply to the right into a steep, boulder-strewn pass. "I hope I remember the directions correctly," he added, and not very reassuringly, as they turned into another steep-walled ravine, then another.

"Right, left, right, right, right, left, left, up and over—"

And with that they passed over a granite ridge and into a lake-filled valley.

"There it is," said the griffin.

Patrick looked to where the beast was aiming his massive beak. A sweeping line—too flat and even to be a natural piece of geography—arced across the darkened valley floor. The griffin descended and began to follow the crumbling ties and rusted steel rails of the train tracks, which, maybe two miles distant, disappeared into the mouth of a narrow, crudely hewn tunnel.

They were skimming maybe just a hundred yards above the rails when the griffin pulled in his wings, and Patrick's stomach leapt into his throat. He had that weightless roller-coaster sensation and suddenly felt like he had to pee. Oma jolted awake and dug her fingers into Patrick's sides, screaming like she was falling off a cliff.

"It's okay," Patrick yelled, hoping it really was. The ground was coming up so fast he wondered if My-Chale maybe couldn't see it because he wasn't slowing at all and—

The griffin back-flapped his wings, throwing up a cloud of gravel and dirt that made the world disappear. Then all was still, other than the sound of pebbles raining down.

"Sorry about that, Oma," My-Chale said as he straightened up and gave a big sneeze. "Let's hurry inside. Sun will be up soon."

"So we're staying in a train tunnel today, huh?" said Patrick, sliding off the griffin's back and pulling the skin-suit hood up over his face to filter the dust.

"Beats a drainage ditch," said Oma, coughing as she slid down next to him.

Yesterday they'd slept inside a storm culvert running under an abandoned highway. It had been pretty damp, cramped, and smelly. When the sun was up, it was necessary to hide from the sky and its many, many cameras—the Deacons' "sky-eyes," as they called them here.

"Yes, I suppose this will be deluxe in comparison," said My-Chale. He swept his head back and forth, looking for something on the ground. "And you'll enjoy the company, too."

"Company?" asked Patrick.

"Ah, here," said the big griffin.

Patrick and Oma came over to look.

In small white painted letters along the inside of the left rail was a message, just visible in the moonlight. Patrick couldn't make out what it said, but Oma's big eyes apparently had a slightly easier job of it.

Nothing can cure the soul but the senses, just as nothing can cure the senses but the soul.

"A classic," said Oma.

"Yes, it is that," said My-Chale.

"Tonight's marker?" asked Patrick.

My-Chale nodded. Similar quotes from *The Book of Commonplace* had been left at their past two hideouts, too.

"Hey, what's that light?" asked Oma. Her big eyes were trained down the tunnel ahead of them.

Off in the darkness, a pulsing green-yellow light brightened and soundlessly grew.

"What do you think it is?" asked My-Chale. The playful tone to his voice told Patrick and Oma they shouldn't be alarmed. "What do your eyes and your ears tell you?"

Patrick figured the thing either had to be growing or coming closer, or both. Since it was absolutely steady, not bobbing or swaying in the slightest, it seemed to him it either was riding on the train rails or somehow floating. It didn't seem to be electrical, either—it wasn't like looking at headlights or bulbs or even at a screen. The edges were blurry and round-seeming somehow. Maybe it was some sort of glow-in-the-dark gas. It sure was quiet, whatever it was.

"A cloud of lightning bugs," said Patrick.

"What are *lightning bugs*?" asked Oma.

"You know—fireflies?"

"Wha-at?" said Oma.

"You know—in the summer you see them glowing out in the yard."

"I don't think we get those in our yard," said Oma.

"There are no more lightning bugs," said My-Chale. "The Deacons killed all non-useful insects in the years after the Purge. What's your guess, Oma?"

"It's some sort of vapor," she replied. "You'd let us know if we should be worried, right?"

"No need to worry," said the griffin.

"It's not radioactive?" said Patrick.

Oma laughed.

The thing was by now filling the entire tunnel entrance and had stopped advancing.

"Let's go right to the source," said My-Chale. "How would you describe yourself, Laurence?" A fuzzy slit appeared in the middle of the glowing cloud and moved like a mouth.

"I suppose they call me a will-o'-the-wisp," said the rather thoughtful-sounding voice that emerged.

CHAPTER 4

Strange Dreams

L ISTEN," SAID LUCIE, PUTTING DOWN THE CHARCOAL.
Her portrait of Mr. BunBun just wasn't working out. It
was more a big dumb guinea pig with antlers than a miraculous, sparkly-eyed, talking jackalope.

"We can't just sit around like this. We need a plan."

Neil looked up from the computer screen. They'd been
through this before. There simply wasn't anything they could
do. If they searched the Internet for information they shouldn't
know, the bad people would see. If they contacted others, tried
to draw attention to these things they shouldn't know, the bad
people would hear.

The Griffin kids weren't supposed to know their brother

Patrick was alive on another world. And then they definitely weren't supposed to know of the man who had taken over that world already and was now trying to take over Earth. His name was Rex Abraham, and he was planning to kill everybody over the age of three and then to re-carpet the world with a new micromanaged high-tech monoculture.

They also weren't supposed to have met the talking jackalope named Mr. BunBun who was here trying to save the Earth.

The whole situation was really, really frustrating. And also pretty scary.

"Right," said Neil to his eldest sister. "So what's the big idea that doesn't get us—" he broke off to make sure the Twins weren't looking and then drew his finger across his throat.

"The dreams," Lucie replied.

For the past few nights, the six of them, the Twins included, had been having vivid dreams featuring fantastic creatures. They weren't typical dreams that you half-remembered and then soon forgot. These were dreams that stuck with you throughout the next day when you were fully awake. And they weren't nightmares. They actually—even for the often cynical older Griffin children—left an impression of joy and wonder.

Lucie kept being visited by an enormous griffin. Eva, a giant backpacking woman. Neil had dreamed of a giant talking squid (it wasn't unusual for him to dream of squids, he explained, just talking ones) and also a floating ball of light that lived in a cave. Carly had dreamed of baby anteaters who traveled in packs and spoke with one voice. And the Twins claimed to have variously been dreaming of dinosaurs, monkeys, camels, and "mammoths with people's arms."

The fact that Mr. BunBun had predicted these dreams only increased their trust in the other things he'd said.

He had explained that these dreams were caused by creatures who, like him, were from a world past Earth and Ith. It was a place called Mindth, and it had once had tremendous influence over the other two worlds.

Rex, apparently, hadn't yet invaded Mindth, and was trying to contain its influence. This is why he'd wiped the Mindthlings out on Earth. And was now about to do the same on Ith.

"So Rex doesn't like you guys from Mindth interfering?" Lucie had asked.

BunBun had touched his moist nose. "Yes, that's the crux of it."

"But then why did he leave you alive on Ith?" Eva had asked.

"Yeah," Lucie had said. "Didn't you say he killed off everybody over the age of three and then remade things the way he liked them? Why would he kill these Mindthlings off on Earth, where he doesn't have full control, but leave you alive on Ith, where he does?"

BunBun replied that he didn't fully understand it himself but it appeared to be part of a strategy to take over *all three* of the worlds. Part of it might have to do with public relations—by keeping a very few Mindthlings alive on Ith, he was giving the young government somebody to blame for anything bad that happened.

But also, he believed, Rex might be experimenting. Mindth, BunBun explained, was very different from Earth and Ith. Earth was the world of hearing. Ith was the land of sight. And

Mindth—at least in the ideal—was the land of dreams, and of understanding.

But understanding can be clouded by confusion. BunBun said many believed that if the good residents of Mindth were able to see past Rex's deceptions, they might somehow rally to stop him. Somehow Rex was keeping Mindth disconnected.

Mindth had always been the most mysterious of the three worlds. Even Mindthlings like BunBun didn't have a clear picture of the place. He himself could recall nothing about how it looked, or what the weather was like, or even who he'd known there.

This is where Lucie got to thinking.

"Neil," she said, "go to Google Trends."

"What's that?" asked Neil.

"Whatever people look up in Google, they keep track of the words they search and graph how much they're used."

"This?" said Neil, pointing at the screen.

"Yes," said Lucie. "Now type in 'dream' in the box."

"Okay," said Neil. A wavy blue line popped up showing that over the past dozen years there had been a general decrease in searches that involved the word *dream*.

"That's by month," observed Lucie. "Bring it just to the past seven days in the menu up top."

Neil did as she said and they saw that over the past five days there had been a huge and steadily increasing rise in people searching the word.

"So," said Neil, "a lot more people than usual are searching *dream* lately. And your point is . . ."

"It's happening because *everybody*'s been having freaky dreams," said Eva. "And so they've been looking it up online."

"Because the *Internet*'s a good place to get your dreams explained," said Neil sarcastically.

"I didn't say it was a good idea, but people do look stuff up they don't understand, right?" said Lucie. "Obviously not everybody's googling 'I had a strange dream,' but if, like, one in fifty people does, then that still is a lot more than usual, right? Don't you see—it's proof of what BunBun said about how we and a lot of people would be hearing from that other world in our dreams."

"And so," said Neil, "that somehow gives us a plan?"

"Yes," said Lucie. "Yes it does."

CHAPTER 5
Return of the King

REX ABRAHAM HAD NEVER ENJOYED THE TRAN-
substantiation process. Part of it was the matter of
control. You never had any idea precisely where on the other
world (Ith, in this case) you would arrive. And then there was
the entire loss-of-consciousness issue. He'd tried with all his
might to stay awake and focused, but the physics of the situation were clearly too much for a human mind, even an augmented one like his own. You came through the other end
unconscious and with your senses fuzzy and overloaded, forced
to concentrate all your effort on regaining sight, hearing, even
your sense of balance.

He fought through the swirling vertigo and stood, growling with anger as his eyes focused on a piece of graffiti on the wall of a derelict building:

> *Always to be right, always to trample forward, and never to doubt, are not these the great qualities with which dullness takes the lead in the world?*
> *—W. M. Thackeray BCP §1859303*

And then, in the same spray-painted handwriting,

> *WELCOME, REX ABRAHAM! BE SURE TO REGISTER YOURSELF WITH THE BUREAU OF MICROMANAGEMENT WITHIN TEN MINUTES OF YOUR ARRIVAL!*

Mindthlings had clearly left the messages. They had been composed in archaic written English rather than in Ith's vastly more efficient thirty-seven-letter phonetic alphabet. Also, regular Ithlings would never have referenced minutes, which had been replaced by Rex's new decimal timekeeping system of dunts, terts, quats, and quints.

He applied some hand sanitizer (he'd been forced to touch his palms to the ground in standing up) and activated the geo-positioning app in his cerebral computer. Rex, and some of his higher-ranking ministers, had implants.

He considered the writing in front of him. He knew it was meant to mock. A feeble attempt at psychological warfare. But the important thing to realize was the writer had known Rex was arriving from Earth at this very spot.

Objectively, he was confident the enemy had no more understanding of transubstantiation physics than he did. If they had, *he* would be the one on the run, and *they* would be the ones about to seize complete control of Earth and Ith.

He flashed his perfect white teeth as it occurred to him how badly they had failed to capitalize on the situation. Knowing where and when he was coming, they could have prepared a trap and at least tried to kill him. But all they'd done was leave a sarcastic sign.

It didn't justify his time or energy to think about it a moment longer.

He checked the time stamp and some other metrics on his freshly rebooted retinal display. After briefly taking in the distinctive profile of Mount Fuji in the distance, he activated his cerebral satellite uplink.

First he tapped into a live high-definition sat-cam feed. It was what the technicians called the "god's-eye view," although, of course, nobody in his organization was so naive as to believe in any god.

From the crystal-clear fringes of outer space, the vapor trails of six supersonic emergency-response aircraft were raking across the Sea of Japan.

He uncoupled the feed and held his BNK-E out in front of him.

A holograph materialized in the air above the device's

flexible screen. The Seer's wide-cheeked, heavily made-up—and obviously shocked—face stared back at him.

"Your Observantness," he said crisply to the startled woman. Ith's oldest human and its revered leader, the Seer, stammered and put a hand to her lipsticked mouth, apparently to prevent herself from spluttering.

He offered her a less-than-reassuring smile.

"Your Awarenence!" she blurted. "*You're* the incoming tran-sub at 139.75—"

"Degrees east, yes. Please instruct your interceptors not to shoot on sight. And get my compound ready. I'll be heading straight there and will expect a briefing on how long it will take to remediate the remaining Mindthlings. They've run wild long enough. And we're going to need a lot of transcense in the coming days."

CHAPTER 6
Freaky Squid Dreams

LOOK," LUCIE CONTINUED. "IT'S WEIRD THAT THERE isn't more coverage about Patrick, right?"

Eva and Carly both shrugged. Neil shook his head. It seemed to him there had been more than a lot of attention for their missing brother. There had been reporters at the house. And 10 News Westchester was still running the story every few hours. An Amber Alert had been issued. And Mom's Facebook page had been entirely mobbed with supportive, emotion-filled comments from friends and strangers alike.

Somebody had even taken Patrick's class picture from last year and made a *FIND PATRICK* meme that people were using as a profile picture.

But there was no question: five days after Patrick had gone missing, the public interest was waning.

"I checked what the FBI investigator said, and it's true," said Neil. "On average, more than a thousand children are reported missing in the United States every single day."

"Most are safely found," said Lucie.

Neil conceded the point with a shrug.

"I bet it's just a few that go missing for more than a day," she went on. "And only maybe a couple dozen disappear completely each year."

"So?" said Neil, a good dose of gotcha to his voice. "Do you hear a couple dozen stories about kids who go permanently missing? I don't."

"Sure you do," said Lucie. "Like Amber of the Amber Alerts. Or like that girl who was the pageant star whose father they think did it."

"Or like that boy from Seattle that was in Mom's *People* magazine," said Carly. "The one whose mom is president of that company."

"You see?" said Lucie.

"Doesn't sound like dozens to me," said Neil.

"I bet most of the kids who go permanently missing that we don't hear about aren't from Westchester," said Lucie. "And probably aren't white."

"That's racist," said Eva.

"I'm not the racist one," said Lucie.

"Well, I'm no racist," said Neil.

"Society's racist," said Lucie. "Don't you see? A rich, white, suburban kid going missing like this should be making bigger news than this."

"*That* is racist," said Neil.

"It's not racist, it's reality," said Lucie.

"We're not rich," said Carly. "Polly Fettridge is rich."

"In the grand scheme of things we *are* rich," said Lucie. "And the media—which is watched, paid for, and mostly made up of people just like us—would normally be giving more attention to a missing boy like Patrick."

"All right," said Neil. "So what are we going to do? Call the reporters racist snobs, and then they're going to pay attention and figure out that what that rabbit told us is all true and the world will be saved and Patrick will come back?"

"You said you had a plan, Luce," said Eva. "That had to do with our dreams?"

"Yes," said Lucie. "I was just pointing out the press situation because I think it's part of the pattern BunBun was telling us about. He told us we can't go warn people about this Rex Abraham person because they might come for us. And we can't talk about BunBun because they might come for us. But not only that—not only is there danger for ourselves—but even if we *did* manage to get the attention of some reporters, I bet the story wouldn't get out there. I bet it would be kept quiet."

"So there's no point trying anything, but still you have a plan?" said Neil.

"Yes, I think there's one thing we can do," said Lucie.

"What one thing?" asked Neil.

"BunBun didn't tell us we couldn't talk about dreams.

People have dreams, right? And people can talk about dreams, right? There's nothing illegal or even unusual about that, is there?"

"Well, it's not exactly normal," said Neil.

"Don't you see? That's how we can at least talk to Mom and Dad. Just ask them if they've had any weird dreams. And maybe let's start looking around for people online who are posting about having weird dreams. BunBun told us when people go from one world to the other—like he and Patrick have—that people all around often have these dreams, right? Like the griffin I told you I dreamed about who told me that Patrick was safe?"

"Oh," said Neil, nodding for the first time in days. "Or like the squid I dreamed about that told me to get on an airplane to Texas."

"Because, you're saying," said Eva, "if everybody is having these weird dreams, then maybe some of us are getting the same messages and—"

"You're pretty smart sometimes, Luce," said Neil, turning back to the computer screen. "So, you think if we start searching around for people posting about their dreams—maybe just search 'Freaky squid dream'—we'll find some clues or at least connect with people and—oh . . ."

"What is it, Neil?" asked Carly.

"Check this out—lohud.com is reporting a bear sighting in the Bronx."

"When?" asked Lucie, coming over to look at the screen.

"Just about an hour ago," replied Neil. "A jogger took a picture."

"See that?!" said Lucie, gesturing at a smudgy brown shape, basically discernible as an animal hurrying through the still-leafless gray woods.

"Looks like a 'squatch picture," said Carly, a regular viewer of *Finding Bigfoot* on television.

"That's no bear," said Neil.

"Deer Rabbit!" said Cassie and Paul, who had abandoned their plastic toys to join their older siblings in front of the computer.

"That's him, isn't it?" asked Carly.

"It's totally the right size," said Lucie. "Though he's on all fours, not standing like when we saw him."

"If it's supposed to be a black bear, why is it brown in the picture?" said Carly.

"They get into that in the article," said Neil. "Apparently black bears have different color phases. But, wait—listen to this, 'One of the two joggers, Karen Torres of Riverside, said at first she was so startled she thought it was a giant rabbit.'"

"It's the Bronx," said Eva. "He *said* he was going to New York City."

"*Dinosaur* museum," said little Paul, putting down his toy mastodon and looking at Lucie. Cassie's and his favorite place on Earth was the American Museum of Natural History. As far as they were concerned, New York City existed solely to contain it.

"Deer Rabbit is going there today," said Cassie. Deer Rabbit was what the two of them called Mr. BunBun.

Paul nodded emphatically. "We dreamed it," he and Cassie said to Lucie at almost the same time.

"Okay, that's a little creepy," Neil whispered to Carly. She elbowed him sharply in the ribs.

"What?" he whispered.

"Don't be a jerk, Neil," said Lucie. "You guys dreamed of Deer Rabbit at the museum, huh?"

Cassie and Paul nodded emphatically.

"This is *cray*-zee," said Carly, flopping back on the bed dramatically.

"Yeah, well, it is crazy sitting here doing *nothing*," said Neil. "So your big plan, Luce, was to google for people having weird dreams and see if Mom and Dad have been having them?"

"Yes, for starters," said Lucie. "And another idea just occurred to me, too: let's offer to take the Twins to the museum."

The Twins took the sentence as statement more than suggestion and squealed with delight.

"Seriously?" asked Neil.

"I'm seventeen. And Eva, Carly, and you will help. We can ride in on the train. It'll let Mom and Dad chill a bit not having us here in the house all day."

"Didn't BunBun tell us to stay home?" asked Eva. "I mean, I don't see what the harm would be, but—"

"Is it *his* brother, or *our* brother, that's missing here?" asked Lucie. "Come on, guys, what do you say?"

The Twins were by now jumping up and down.

"Beats staying cooped up in here another day," said Neil, shrugging.

Eva nodded, too.

"And," Lucie said, "who knows? Maybe if we actually run into Mr. BunBun again—"

"This is the weirdest week of my *entire* life," said Carly, putting her hands on the sides of her head as she got up off Lucie's bed and followed her siblings out of her sister's room and down the stairs.

CHAPTER 7

Deadball Physics

LAURENCE, LAURENCE NIGHTINGALE," SAID THE glowing cloud with a voice like a swarm of electric mosquitoes.

"I'm Oma. Nice to meet you, Laurence."

"And I'm, uh, Patrick Griffin," said Patrick, trying to decide where to most politely focus his eyes and then wondering if there was going to be some sort of handshake—or elbow-bump, as was the convention on Ith. The creature had neither hands nor elbows.

"Laurence is one of our best healers, and a talented philosopher to boot," said My-Chale.

"It's all true," said the cloud, deadpan sarcasm evident

despite the fuzziness of its voice. "I'm highly awesome. But, here, let's hold any further discussion until we're deeper inside the tunnel. The eyes," it said, extending a tentacle-like appendage and gesturing upward, "they are aloft."

The cloud, without appearing to turn around, ushered them inside the tunnel, casting enough light on the walls and railbed that the three visitors were able to find their way.

"There's a bit of an antechamber ahead, where I've done my best to make things homey," it said.

"I'm sure it will be wonderful," said My-Chale.

"We slept in a storm sewer last night," said Oma. "We're pretty easy."

"Well, yes, it will be better than a sewer. There it is up ahead on the right," it said, coalescing a piece of itself into something of a flashlight and shining a beam into a side passage.

"Laurence!" said My-Chale as he stepped into the false tunnel, "You shouldn't have—"

The will-o'-the-wisp's light had revealed two well-made beds and an enormous pile of straw built up like a giant bird's nest.

"Did I get the bedding right, My-Chale? I seem to recall you enjoy sleeping on dead reeds."

"Yes—though I haven't done so in years. You really are very thoughtful—"

"I get this one," said Oma, rushing forward to claim the queen-sized bed in the middle, leaving Patrick with the smaller one closest to the chamber's entrance.

"I wanted this one anyhow," said Patrick, taking a seat.

"Now," said My-Chale, crouching upon his pile of straw as Laurence floated up to the chamber's vaulted ceiling, "tell us what's been happening, Laurence. Is Edna keeping courage? And have there been any updates on Operation Nine Ball?"

"Edna's ready to do it, if and when we need her, and yes indeed, there's an update on Operation Nine Ball."

"And?" My-Chale's voice seemed strained.

"Well . . . it worked," said the glowing cloud.

"It *did*?" asked My-Chale.

"What worked?" asked Oma.

"You remember how Patrick and I dreamed of Rex's arrival?" My-Chale asked. "Well, some of the other Commonplacers had had similar dreams even before that, presaging his arrival."

"Wait, you knew he would be coming?" asked Patrick.

"More like we had a hunch. And, more than that, we also had a notion *where* he would be arriving. The dream was very specific—there was a distinctive landmark, a famous mountain that guided us to the specific location."

"So," said Patrick, thinking through the implications. "What did you do? Put a bomb there?"

"The Deacons use bombs; we don't," My-Chale reminded him.

"So, what then?" asked Oma.

"You recall how transubstantiation works?" asked My-Chale. "How a sentient entity of equal or equivalent mass will be displaced by the arriving entity?"

"Like how I was replaced by your agent—"

"BunBun," said My-Chale.

"How I came here because I was about the same size as BunBun," said Patrick.

"And in the right place," said My-Chale.

"You know the game of pool?" said Laurence the glowing cloud.

Patrick nodded but Oma shook her head. "What's that?"

"Or billiards perhaps? A game played with hard balls on a felt-covered table? The object is often to bounce the balls into each other and cause them to fall into holes around the edge of the table."

"That sounds pretty pointless," said Oma.

"Rex thought so, too," said My-Chale. "It was not one of the games brought back after the Purge."

Oma still looked skeptical.

"It's actually kind of fun," said Patrick. His friend Dexter had a pool table in his basement and Dexter's parents didn't let him use any screens during the day, so they'd actually played quite a lot, at least when the weather wasn't good. Dexter had not just a pool table but also an actual pool, so in the summer, obviously they preferred that.

"Well," said Laurence, "have you ever seen one ball hit another and perfectly take its place—actually come to a dead stop where the previous ball had been?"

Oma shrugged but Patrick nodded.

"It's called a 'deadball shot.' And in this analogy it can only happen if the balls are the same size."

Patrick and Oma both shrugged.

"Okay," said Oma. "So, this is how transubstantiation works?"

"Yes," said Laurence. "If we were to think of it in terms of classical physics (which it isn't quite), the momentum has to be entirely offset. So, if the balls are different sizes, it doesn't work."

"As a woman of science once observed," commented My-Chale, "nothing in this universe is larger, more inflexible, and harder to discover than its rules."

"Huh," said Oma thoughtfully.

"Huh," said Patrick confusedly.

"So," continued Laurence, "that's transubstantiation. The incoming ball—or person—we call the 'transubstantiator.' He or she or it is the one who initiates the process. And we refer to the person of the same mass who is sent back the other way as the 'transubstantiatee.'

"And there's generally no predicting the details of the transubstantiator's arrival—neither who they're going to replace, nor where."

"So, with Rex coming from Earth," said Oma, "you were able to place somebody so that they got knocked back to Earth in Rex's place."

"And not just leave it to random chance," said Laurence. "That's correct."

"But why didn't you just ambush him?" asked Patrick. "If not a bomb, why not just have a bunch of people waiting for him and lock him up?"

"He's so powerful, we would have to have sent a small army," said Laurence.

"And all we *have* is a small army, a *very* small army," explained My-Chale.

40

"All of the Commonplacers together would have trouble filling a movie theater," said Laurence. "And, if we'd sent any number of us out to the same place under the skies of Ith," he said, again making a glowing gesture upward, "they'd have us all in one fell swoop, as opposed to the current system of picking us off one by one."

"So, again, I know it's against your beliefs," said Patrick, "but Rex kills people. Rex kills *a lot* of people. Wouldn't you be saving a lot more lives if you had just left a big bomb there and killed him? Just one death to save a lot more from happening."

"Or, better yet," said My-Chale somberly, "couldn't we avoid every piece of pain and sadness coming in the future if we undertook the momentary discomfort of killing ourselves?"

"What do you mean?" asked Patrick. "Suicide?"

"It's the same logic you're using to say that killing makes sense," said Oma.

"What?"

"Think it through, Earthling," said Laurence.

Patrick did think it through. And it still seemed pretty different to him. Killing yourself was one thing. Killing a bad person to prevent him from killing a lot of other people was an entirely different concept.

"Look," said Patrick, trying to explain his thoughts. "The future also contains good things. I mean, if you kill yourself, you don't get any of that, either."

"So, killing yourself," said My-Chale, "essentially gets you what?"

"Nothing," said Patrick. "It gets you nothing."

"Don't you see? The *yourself* part isn't what matters," said Oma. "It's killing. Killing brings the world *nothing*. Period."

"'O grave, where is thy victory?'" quipped Laurence.

"That's from *The Book of Commonplace*," said Oma.

"Among the very first entries," said My-Chale, somehow seeming to smile despite his inflexible beak.

Patrick was impressed by the conversation but still was not convinced. "So you guys are, like, pacifists," he said.

"Yes," said Laurence, a note of deadpan sarcasm again detectable in his diffuse voice, "pacifists who *fight* all day long."

"We aren't against violence in the face of oppression," said My-Chale.

"In fact we're quite fond of violence," said Laurence, swirling and getting kind of flickery as he spoke. "Violence of expression, violence of thought, violence against the lies of those who would stifle our minds and senses!"

"But we won't kill," said Oma.

"Killing's backward," said My-Chale. "Taking a life—however logically justifiable it may seem—is subtracting from the universe, not adding to it."

Patrick decided he'd try to sort this all out later. He was too tired to keep thinking on it now.

"So," said Oma, "you got somebody close to Rex's arrival point. And they're now on Earth, helping BunBun."

"Precisely," said My-Chale. "Only it wasn't somebody; it was *somebodies*."

"We had another hunch, you see," explained Laurence. He had calmed down and wasn't so flickery any longer. "It needn't be one sentient entity of the same mass but could in fact be several who *add up to* an equivalent mass. Provided they are touching each other."

"Okay—so you sent more than one person back in Rex's place," said Patrick.

"So, little children?" asked Oma.

"Numbats," said My-Chale.

"The nine numbats," said Laurence, as if that were self-explanatory.

CHAPTER 8
Pet Shop Noise

SVEN, **TENTY, DIRTY, SHORTY, SHIFTY, TRIXY,** Levanty, Graty, and Barb grabbed one another and rolled around, laughing like little maniacs, in the middle of the floor.

"It worked! It worked!" yelled Graty.

"Let go, Shorty. We don't need to be touching any longer!" shouted Tenty.

"I can't believe it!" said Dirty.

"I'm going to sneeze," replied Levanty, and then she did, three times.

"I can't breathe," said Barb, who had somehow gotten shoved to the very bottom of the pile. Still, she wasn't exactly unhappy they had finally transubstantiated. All that waiting around had been driving her crazy.

They'd been holding hands in that abandoned train station for nearly five dunts before it finally happened.

Three nights ago, Shifty, who was as talkative in the morning as she was all day long, had described to the rest of them an intensely vivid dream she'd had. She'd been in an abandoned, falling-apart old train station. She knew it had to be in Japan because she had seen Mount Fuji in the distance. And she'd been holding hands in a circle with all of her brothers and sisters. And then there had been a big green flash. And then Rex Abraham himself had been there.

"What?!" Shifty had asked, seeing that all eight of her siblings had stopped chewing their cereal to stare at her. "What are all of you guys looking at?!"

"I had the very same dream!" Graty had replied.

"Me, too," said Sven, and then Tenty, Levanty, Barb, and the rest of them. They'd gone and told Purse-Phone, their local Commonplace librarian, immediately.

Purse-Phone, a giant who was fond of hiking, explained that when a dream like that happens—when it's shared by more than one dreamer— it's more than a regular dream; it's a message from Mindth. And, often enough, it's not just a message, but instructions.

In this case, the message appeared to be that they had a chance to be transubstantiated to Earth. And that meant that they had a chance—as BunBun had—to save that imperiled world.

So she had each memorize BunBun's message for Earth

and recite it back dozens of times. And then she'd sent them off to search through the ruins of Japan, where they finally found the train station from their dream, camped out, and (this was the toughest part) held hands for nearly half a day. Purse-Phone surmised that they had to be physically touching in order to form a mass equivalent to Rex's. And now, well, here they were on Earth!

"Okay, great, we did it. Now, where the hockey puck are we?" asked Sven.

"We're in a *pet shop!*" shouted Dirty. His observation was shortly emphasized by a chorus of caged animals—yipping, yowling, chirping, squawking—as their initial fright wore off.

"Look how big that lizard is!" said Tenty, standing up on her hind legs and staring into the terrarium next to her. Unlike the parrots, kittens, and puppies, the reptile didn't seem particularly interested in them.

"It's a monitor," said Barb not very loudly, since she knew nobody was going to pay her any attention anyhow. Although they were numbats—albeit sentient ones from Mindth that were about ten times bigger than the average wild numbat—the rest of them didn't give an owl's butt about nature. They didn't even know that wild numbats were small termite-eating marsupials native to Australia. All they knew was that they were brothers and sisters and that they were from Mindth. Though they didn't remember anything about it.

"I've read about pet shops in books," said Shifty.

"Me, too," said Trixy, looking thoughtful. "Boy, that would *so* suck."

"What?" asked Levanty.

"To be trapped in here and then somebody comes and sticks *us* in a cage and we're sold off to different families and never get to complete our mission and—"

"I don't think people have numbats for *pets*," said Barb.

"Why not?" asked Trixy.

"We're cute," said Sven.

"And personable," said Tenty.

"And, hello, very rare and probably highly *endangered*," said Barb.

"What's that got to do with it?" asked Graty.

"I don't see any humans here," said Shorty. "The shop appears to be closed."

"That's because it's the middle of the night," said Levanty, pointing her snout at the darkened window down at the far end of the shop.

"We should figure out where we are," said Barb. "I mean, *other* than in a pet shop."

"Agreed," said Sven. "We can't very well tell where we're going if we don't know where we are."

"Phinneas Feathers' Pet Shop, Towson, Maryland, United States of America," said Trixy, looking at the screen of the binky strapped to Shorty's back. Shorty was the biggest and strongest of them. Only the Nine found his name funny, however, as to most humans and others they all appeared to be pretty much the same size.

"Are you on Earth's Interverse?" asked Dirty.

"They call it an Inter*net* here," said Trixy.

"Well, that's stupid," said Barb. "What, do they catch butterflies with it?"

"Or fish, maybe," said Levanty, staring into a tank of neon tetras.

"Quiet, you guys, every moment we're logged on is another moment Rex's stooges can find us," said Sven. "Trixy—have you searched for BunBun? Any hits?"

"Nope. Nothing."

"And no sign of recent societal upheaval or revolution or anything like that? *Worldwide*, that is?"

"Umm, nope."

"Okay," said Sven. "Well, either BunBun's still safe or he's not, but either way clearly he hasn't completed his mission yet. Which means we are still on the hook for completing ours and need to get ourselves to the nearest major metropolitan area PDQ. What do you see, Trixy?"

"Well, there's a place called Baltimore that we're real close to, but just a bit farther there's this huge star on the map—Washington, DC, it's called. Let's see . . . apparently the star means it's a capital."

"Like Silicon City back on Ith?" asked Tenty.

"What's the DC stand for?" asked Levanty.

"Death Central," said Barb glumly.

"Shh," said Dirty. "It doesn't matter. It's where we need to go."

"Okay, find us a route to get there."

"I've got it all figured out," said Trixy.

"Let's blow this pop stand and get moving!" said Dirty.

"Follow me!" said Sven, and took off down the aisle toward the store's entrance, which, to their collective chagrin, was locked.

CHAPTER 9
Lazarus Inbound

OLD ICHABOD COFFIN, FRESH FROM THE HOSPITAL
after his traumatic home invasion, had found the same
online LoHud.com story about the jogger who saw the bear. It
was reposted all over Facebook.

"That's no bear, you morons!" he said, instantly recogniz-
ing the furry shape despite the terrible quality of the cell-phone
picture, and the still-watering, blurry condition of his own
eyes. "That's a drug-addicted criminal!"

He sat forward and stared at the most recent Facebook responses.

OMG. I'm never going jogging on the Rockefeller
trails again!
Okay, my Giuseppe is SO becoming an indoors-
only cat.
And you thought the Bronx was unsafe before—
LOL!!!
I'm generally against hunting but, you know . . .

"What a bunch of idiots!" he yelled, clearly practiced in conversing with himself in an empty room. "Can't you see that that's not a bear?! First of all, it's light brown, not black. We don't get grizzlies on the East Coast. Second, look how it's moving! Bears don't run like that—the proportions are all wrong. And the *reason* they're wrong is that's not a *bear*; it's a *drug-addicted vandal*!

"I mean," he said, continuing in a modulated voice. "I'll admit it's a very, very good costume. When he burgled *my* house I was, at first, completely taken in."

He grew angry all over again remembering the patronizing policewoman who had interviewed him at the hospital. Despite the abundant physical evidence—the knocked-over bird-feeder, the mocking business cards, the drowned phones— she kept asking if any valuables had been taken and if anybody might be mad at him. Had he had any misunderstandings, trouble with money, lawsuits, disagreements with family or friends?

She had seemed bent on turning the focus to him when obviously there was a sick-in-the-head criminal still on the loose! A sick-in-the-head criminal who had flooded his kitchen and destroyed a six-hundred-dollar iPhone!

He needed to go to the Apple Store today and get a replacement.

He harrumphed as another credulous post appeared in the "Bronx Bear" conversation.

With this kind of bear is it best to play dead, or to try to scare it away? I always get mixed up. 😛

He clicked away and looked up the train schedule. He'd ride into Manhattan, replace his phone at the Apple Store, and get lunch at his favorite restaurant. No question he'd had a horrible few days and deserved a treat.

He went to the back hall, grabbed his wallet, the keys to his Mercedes, an umbrella in case it rained, and his portable can of Mace. He always carried personal protection when traveling in the city.

A blue jay was making angry noises outside and he looked out the back-door window. His feeders were filled but there were no birds at them, which seemed strange till he saw a hideous old alley cat—its fur clumpy with age—huddled on the ground, its crooked tail flicking from side to side.

Old Mr. Coffin hurried outside brandishing his can of Mace. The cat gave him the briefest devil-eyed stare before turning and taking flight.

"What is the world coming to?" he shouted as the animal disappeared into the early-spring woods. "Drug addicts in our kitchens, stray cats in our yards? Is there no more law and order at all?"

The first call he was going to make on his new phone would be to the animal control bureau.

CHAPTER 10
Iron Mind, Tired Bladder

PATRICK SAT UP IN HIS BED, BLINKING AROUND
the dim room, expecting to be disoriented, but somehow
he wasn't. He knew he was inside a train tunnel. He knew the
sound of crashing surf was actually a griffin snoring atop a
pile of straw. He knew the source of the wobbling green light
was a glowing ball of gas named Laurence. It was a bizarre
scene, yet somehow reassuring.

The only thing that gave him any apprehension was perhaps the least unusual player in the scene: the runaway Ithling girl with the big eyes in the bed across from his.

Not like Oma weirded him out or anything; it was just that
he found himself unable to *not* think about her. It was like

she was a big magnet and his brain was filled with iron filings, and whenever she was nearby, all his thoughts crammed up against the side of his skull closest to her.

There were worse situations, he knew. It was better, for instance, thinking about her than it was dwelling on how badly he needed to pee.

They'd gotten used to the lack of plumbing on their cross-country journey—ducking into woods, going behind buildings, even having My-Chale touch down for unscheduled breaks during their nocturnal flights—but he'd forgotten to relieve himself before going to bed, and there was no way he was getting back to sleep in this condition.

Laurence was an amazing host. He'd given them a dinner of peanut butter on gluten-free bread (which he'd stolen from a URL, an underground supply train), and the beds (which he'd liberated from an old warehouse) were a total luxury after the past few nights of sleeping on the ground. But their host hadn't shown them any kind of toilet, or even a bucket.

Patrick felt for his binky and checked the time. It was almost 2.5 dunts. On Ith, a day was divided into tenths called "dunts," and it began in the morning versus at midnight like it does on Earth. So Patrick (with a little help from the calculator app on his binky) estimated it was about one in the afternoon, Earth-time. Which meant—since they were traveling at night and sleeping by day—he had at least four more hours till everybody woke up.

So he either had to wake people up or go open a lemonade stand—as his brother Neil might say—all on his own. Their father had once observed that Neil had more expressions for peeing than bankers have for loans. "Draining the main vein," "wizzing the lizard," "having an appointment with Dr. Leaky," "undamming the Yellow River," "topping off the toilet tank," and "rolling out the foam carpet," to name just a few.

Patrick looked over at Oma. Her long dark hair was splayed out past the edges of the pillow beneath which she'd buried her head. He swung his legs over the side of the bed, stood on the surprisingly clean stone floor, decided not to put on his foot-gloves, and quietly tiptoed out of the sleeping chamber.

Shifting his weight back and forth because he had to go so badly, Patrick looked both ways down the main tunnel and decided to go left.

He crunched a dozen wincing paces down the gravel-floored train bed and relieved himself against the tunnel wall.

Just as he was finishing up, a breeze began to blow down the tunnel. He resealed the Velcro fly on his ninja suit and started heading back to the sleeping cave. The breeze was really, really blowing, whipping his hair and making him squint.

And now there was a noise, a dull hum and also some sort of regular thumping sound, a thumping sound that was getting pretty loud and that he could feel resonating through the floor. And then there was a flicker of bright blue light down the tunnel ahead of him.

Something was coming. Something big, and something fast. Almost oblivious to the pain of his bare feet on the pointy gravel, he dashed back up the side tunnel that led to where his friends were still sleeping, stopped, and peered around the corner at the approaching whatever-it-was. The light was getting brighter and bluer, like a spotlight, and the thumping noise was sounding more and more like footsteps, the footsteps of something very heavy. He turned and hurried farther down the side tunnel. He needed to get out of sight, he needed to warn them, needed to—

"Ooomf!" he said as something flattened him against the cold rock wall.

CHAPTER 11
Still as the Grave

NOT GOOD, NOT GOOD, NOT GOOD," BUNBUN whispered. There simply weren't any good spots to hide. No culverts, no sewer grates, no old buildings with barbed-wire fences he could hop, no bodies of water with which to mask his tracks.

He could hear his pursuer in the distance still—the high-pitched keening of electronics, the occasional snapping twig. He hoped he'd left a difficult-to-follow trail, leaping in thirty-foot bounds from rocky outcrop to rocky outcrop. But the man (or part-man, part-android, as BunBun had reason to suspect) clearly hadn't given up yet.

BunBun huddled inside a cemetery plot, an overgrown,

hundred-foot-square vault of crumbling, vandalized graves. It was surrounded on three sides by a moldering stone wall, and by an old iron fence on the fourth. He tried his very best to slow his heart rate and breathing. Goodness only knew what his pursuer's high-tech sensors might be able to detect.

He repeated his mantra—the same one he'd used during his transubstantiation—to himself, slowing his racing thoughts, easing his breathing, calming his heartbeat,

"Ears are for Earth,
Eyes are for Ith
And both in their way
Help the true become Truth!"

It began to work. His erect ears collapsed into a relaxed state, and he no longer heard any snapping branches, humming capacitors, or crackling databursts. Soon all he sensed were the strange but not surprising noises of the park sparrows and the big city beyond—the moaning traffic, the thumping garbage containers, the dragonfly-like *whump-whump-whump* of small flying machines . . .

His eyes went wide.

A helicopter-bladed drone, no bigger than a small bat, was flitting about the still-leafless treetops, turning slowly, angling its sensors left and right, sweeping the terrain below, including—presently—the terrain that BunBun occupied.

He gave up his mantra repetitions and held his breath. His furry coat would somewhat help disguise his heat signature.

Hopefully he'd manage not to stand out from the cold, lifeless dirt and stone around him.

"Oh, crud," he said as the drone paused, and—with a little *pok-pok-pok-pok* sound—fired four darts straight down at his upturned face.

CHAPTER 12
Supervisory Capacities

SURE, WHY NOT? RIGHT, MARY?" SAID MR. GRIFFIN, looking down at the big crowd of children gathered at the foot of their bed.

Lucie was pleased. She and the other children had just sprung on their parents the notion of riding the train into the city and taking the Twins to the natural history museum. It was true, Rick Griffin reflected, Lucie and Eva were old enough to be babysitters. And all of the kids had been so marvelous lately. It was a horrible situation, Patrick missing, but it had been great seeing how well the children had been getting along, how mature and helpful they had become. He couldn't recall a single fight or meltdown since Saturday.

"Into the city, all by yourselves?" said Mrs. Griffin, sitting up and putting on the glasses she only ever wore between the bed and her contact lens case in the bathroom. Neil and Eva had never actually seen her wearing them before that moment.

"Those glasses make you look *old*, Mom," said the latter.

"Well, maybe *you* should wear them, then, Eva," said Mrs. Griffin, "because you're not old enough to be taking a couple of four-year-olds into the city."

Mary Griffin was often her sharpest on waking.

"But I checked online," said Neil, "and it's cool—Lucie's seventeen—she's old enough to take kids on the train *and* into the museum. And, if you give us some money for the tickets, we can just walk to the station. You don't even need to give us a ride."

"I used to take my little sisters to the mall when I was younger than they are," said Mr. Griffin.

"That was the eighties," said Mrs. Griffin. "And in Minnesota. Look, you guys, I really appreciate the thought. It's very sweet. But the last thing we need is somebody seeing or even hearing about the rest of my non-missing children wandering around New York City all by themselves. I mean, I'd love for you guys to go off and have some fun, but . . ." Her pillow-creased face brightened suddenly. "Nana!"

"What?" said Neil and Eva almost simultaneously. Carly just nodded, as if she'd been expecting this.

"*Nana* can go with you."

"Nana!" yelled the Twins.

Rick shrugged. His mother-in-law and the kids *both* being out of Mary's hair for the day would definitely be a good thing.

Nana had been at the house every day since Patrick's disappearance, helping with meals, cleaning, drinking wine, and smoking cigarettes on the porch.

Just then there was a chiming sound.

"Is that the front door?" asked Carly.

"Speak of the devil, I'm sure," said Mr. Griffin.

"My mother never rings the doorbell!" said Mrs. Griffin, fussing with her hair and reflexively putting a hand to her glasses.

"This is true," said Rick as he swung his pajamaed legs out of bed and went over to the window.

"*Andrew!?*" he said. "It's your brother Andrew!" He turned to his wife. "Umm, did we know he was coming?"

"*Andrew!?*" said Mrs. Griffin. "He's *here*? At the door?!" She got out of bed and hurried to the window. "No, I mean, we spoke on the phone yesterday, but he didn't say anything about coming up from DC."

"Do you think he brought presents like he usually does?!" said Carly.

The entire family rushed out of the bedroom and down the stairs to greet their favorite uncle.

CHAPTER 13
Tunnel-Striders & Person-Hiders

THERE WAS A WHISPERING IN PATRICK'S EAR, A voice barely recognizable above the rushing mechanical noise coming down the passageway. Laurence's.

"Don't move, don't speak, don't breathe more than you must. I'll do my best to hide you."

Laurence had flattened Patrick against the wall of the side tunnel, just inside the turnoff. Through the gauzy fabric of Laurence's now somehow substantial and no-longer-luminescent body, Patrick could see patches of brightness and shadow playing on the opposite wall. And the bright bits weren't playing nicely. Patrick found himself having to squint.

And now the place was really shaking. Every speck of dust,

drip of water, and piece of falling stone glowed like stars in front of Patrick's face.

Whatever was coming had to be huge.

And then it stomped into sight: a six-legged insect-bodied machine as big as a delivery truck and bristling with antennae. The machine stopped and turned to face Patrick's side tunnel.

Two spotlights swept Patrick's way. He clenched his eyes shut but, even so, the lights were blinding, filling his mind with a brilliant red, then an unearthly white.

And then everything went dark. Patrick opened his eyes. His retinas were stained by the former brightness but he could make out a long, dark-skinned, rubbery appendage snaking toward him. It stopped maybe just a yard away, and a hole opened at its tip. There was a gasping sound as it sucked the air for a full second, then stopped.

The walking machine remained still as this happened, its lights dimming even further. Patrick realized he'd stopped breathing and badly wanted to exhale, but it didn't seem like a good time. He tried to hold it, finding his mind counting the seconds . . . twenty Mississippi, twenty-one Mississippi . . .

He'd once held his breath for sixty-five seconds in Dexter's pool. Just short of Neil's record of sixty-eight seconds.

The machine's lights brightened as it retracted its probe. Another came in its place. This one was skinned with banded metal and tipped with a ball of black plastic foam. It stopped in almost the same place as the first had and made a little puffing sound. A bright blue-purple light lit up the tunnel, and again the big machine fell silent.

. . . fifty-five Mississippi—his mind continued to count as

he fought to keep his chest from heaving out a tired load of air—fifty-six Mississippi, fifty-seven Mississippi, fifty-eight Mississippi, fifty-nine Mississippi, sixty Mississippi—

The purple light flicked off suddenly and all went dark. Sixty-three Mississippi, sixty-four Mississippi, sixty-five Mississippi, sixty-six—

A quiver ran through Laurence, and the machine broke its silence, whining and thumping like somebody had just put a set of fresh batteries into it. Patrick opened his eyes and gasped for air. He'd broken his own breath-holding record (but not Neil's) and now he was going to be killed by a giant metal cave spider.

But the machine wasn't closing in for the kill; it was moving away and continuing down the main tunnel.

"Thank freaking Mindth!" Laurence whispered. Patrick allowed himself a nod and a smile as he enjoyed the sensation of breathing normally.

But then the machine stopped, and Patrick's heart dropped as he realized where it had chosen to pause. It was standing right where he had taken a leak. And now it was sending probes down to inspect the spot, and a red light began to flash atop its carapace.

"Oh, no," said Laurence as the machine began to turn around. And then, to Patrick, he whispered, "Stay very still."

Laurence peeled away from Patrick, re-assumed his glow-ball form, and began hurrying down the main tunnel yelling, "Come on! Can't catch me, you big metal freak!"

The machine swiveled its spotlights on Laurence and began to charge, but as it reached the side tunnel, it halted. One of the spotlights remained trained on Laurence but another swiveled and focused on Patrick.

"Oh," said Patrick, not knowing what to say and feeling in that moment that there was nothing, absolutely nothing, he could do to save himself.

"Over here!" yelled Laurence, imploring the robot. "Come on!"

Then something rushed past Patrick and there was a terrific shriek. The spotlight moved from Patrick to a furry-feathery blur leaping at the robot, which was now extending wicked blades and what looked to be a multi-barreled gun.

CHAPTER 14
Who You Calling a Rat?

ALL WAS GOING AS WELL AS COULD BE EXPECTED aboard the double-decker train to Washington, DC. At least till Shorty got the munchies. For nearly an hour he'd been hiding behind the small garbage receptacle wedged between the middle-most seats. But then a woman getting off at Baltimore-Washington Airport put a half-finished cheese Danish into the bin.

Numbats in the wild are what scientists call myrmecophagic, meaning they have an almost strict diet of termites or ants. Shorty and his eight siblings from Mindth weren't myrmecophagic in the slightest.

Perhaps it came from having much larger brains than normal numbats, but the Nine had tastes that were more human than marsupial, including a love of sweets.

They hadn't had a chance to learn this on Ith because the Deacons had rigorously enforced healthy eating choices—refined sugars, processed fats, and modified flours simply didn't exist on Earth's sister world. And, since the Nine and the other Commonplacers mostly ate food they'd stolen from the Deacons' supply chain, they'd simply never tried any sort of candy, cake, or pastry.

So while Shorty and his siblings had been exploring for another way out of the pet shop (they eventually came across a fan vent above the ceiling tiles and crawled out), they'd chanced upon the owner's small rear office and a stash of snacks that had included a full carton of Twinkies. Which had basically changed their understanding of what food could be.

After devouring the entire stash, they'd felt some remorse and left a note.

Dear Proprietor,

Owe you

· 1 box of Twinkies

· two pretzel braids (we preferred the Twinkies)

· a clean piece of paper just like this one

· the ink dispensed by, and any wear incurred upon, this pen

· any costs associated with letting the garter snakes out of their tank (some of our number wanted to pet them and left the lid unsecured and before we knew it they were all over the place)

Please expect repayment within one month, unless there is a pandemic.

Apologetically yours,
the Nine

For Shorty, who'd always had the biggest appetite of any of them, the Twinkies had been an especially life-changing experience. The sensation of the spongy yellow cake dissolving into ambrosial syrup the second it came in contact with his saliva, the smooth cream filling . . .

Though his overstimulated tongue and the inside of his cheeks felt sore afterward—almost as if they'd been rubbed with very, very fine sandpaper—he had a new obsession.

So, when the early-morning commuter sitting above him had grown tired of her 520-calorie breakfast and tossed it into the very container he'd been resting his head against, he immediately detected the scents of high-fructose corn syrup, partially hydrogenated soybean oil, mono and diglycerides, soy lecithin . . .

It was only a matter of moments before he snapped. He'd still tried to exercise restraint, waiting till she'd gotten up and left before he peered out, looking up and down the aisle to ensure nobody was coming. He'd even checked to make sure that his hiding spot sharer, Tenty, was still asleep. And likewise he had made certain the commuters all around weren't looking his way. Most had gone to sleep, it being still an hour before sunrise. One or two were blearily looking down at screens.

And he of course had been silent as death, padding out into the aisle on the balls of his feet, lifting his toes to ensure his nails didn't clack on the floor even though the roaring of the speeding train would probably have disguised the noise if they had.

But as he removed the plastic-wrapped pastry from the garbage receptacle halfway between the two rows of seats, a woman entered the train car to his left.

She froze stock-still and her eyes went wide as an Ithling's. And she screamed.

"RAT!!!!!!!"

Whereupon Trixy, hiding with Graty behind the garbage container opposite his, peeked around and hissed, "You idiot!!!"

"Icnnnndhpt," he replied, not adequately able to articulate his helplessness through a mouthful of plastic wrapper.

"We need to get downstairs and warn the others to run! NOW!!!" Trixy ordered, bolting down the aisle away from the screaming woman. Graty went right behind her as the entire car exploded in panic.

Not letting go of his sugary prize, Shorty made sure Tenty was with them, and obediently followed.

CHAPTER 15
Breaking Rocks

THE ROBOT'S ROTATING GUN BELCHED A HAIL OF ammunition. With a thunder like a dozen jackhammers going at once, stone shards and bullets ricocheted madly through the tunnel.

Patrick clenched his eyes and pressed himself even harder against the wall. He didn't see what happened next but he sure heard it—a sound of wrenching steel then a world-shuddering crash that caused large sections of the ceiling to come down.

Then all was quiet.

He pulled his head from the wall and looked around. Through a gray haze of throat-stinging dust, he made out what looked like a small thunderstorm by the far wall—flickering tendrils of electricity arcing around it.

As the dust cleared, Patrick saw a severed tentacle lying on the ground like a headless snake and a car-sized slab of rock that had peeled from the tunnel wall. But where was My-Chale?

Patrick's heart dropped.

Laurence returned from down the tunnel and lit up the scene from the right. Oma, stepping past Patrick with her binky, lit up the scene from the left. There—Patrick was relieved to see—was My-Chale, very much alive, his beak filled with a thick tangle of cables and a furious glint in his avian eye.

"You're hurt," said Oma, aiming the light from her binky at a horizontal wound on the griffin's haunch. It wasn't gushing blood, but it was no mere scratch.

"Not as badly as the robot," observed Laurence, gesturing at a puddle of hydraulic fluid on the floor. Patrick was amazed at the utter destruction of the machine. It looked like it had been drop-kicked by a giant and then hit by a train.

My-Chale spat out the wires, lifted his wing, and regarded the wound. "It's nothing."

"Well, let's get it sewn up so it doesn't become something," said Laurence. "My kit's back in the sleeping chamber."

"And then we'd better get out of here," said My-Chale. "I disabled its transponder, though I doubt that any signal could get out from this deep inside the mountain. But they'll notice it's missing before too long."

"What *was* that thing?" asked Patrick.

"I've seen them in my brother's video games," said Oma. "Stalkers or something like that?"

"I think that's what they call them," said My-Chale.

My-Chale was angrier than Patrick had ever seen him. He guessed he might be pretty riled up, too, if he'd just done mortal combat with a killer robot.

"Those machines have killed a lot of us," said Laurence as they made their way back to the sleeping chamber.

"How many?" asked Patrick.

"Well," said Laurence, "there were two thousand and two Mindthlings left alive after Rex's Purge, and there are three hundred eleven of us remaining. Of course we now have about a thousand human recruits, including you and Oma. Which is something."

"Where are they all?" asked Patrick. "Do you have a secret base or something?"

"No main base," said My-Chale, looking away as Laurence looped surgical thread through a needle. "It would be too much of a risk. We have a rule to never gather in numbers greater than eleven. And the humans, most of them, are 'undercover,' as they say in spy books. They are out there in regular Ith society. A very few, just seventy-two now, including Oma, are out in the wilds with us Mindthlings. Hiding underground, moving around as best they can."

"This may pinch a bit," warned Laurence.

"Let's not talk about it, please?" said My-Chale, flinching and keeping his face turned away. Patrick wondered if this massive griffin, leader of the Commonplacers, and fearless slayer of robotic killing machines, might be squeamish about needles.

Laurence somehow gave a glowy shrug despite having no shoulders.

"And Mindthlings," said Patrick. "Oma was telling me, you come from Mindth?"

"Yes," said My-Chale, looking at the far wall as Laurence probed through My-Chale's thick fur and tried to complete the first stitch.

"So, what's Mindth like?"

"You're really hairy, you know," said Laurence. "Can I shave you a bit?"

"You may *not*," said My-Chale, and turned his attention back to Patrick's question. "I can't say that I really remember. None of us can. For me, there was a voice, and there were songs, and there were images, places. But it's like waking from a dream. Trying to remember Mindth is like trying to scoop water with a sieve. You're lucky for whatever drips and drops you get."

"So, when you got here, were you fully grown?" asked Oma.

"He came as an egg, actually," said Laurence.

My-Chale aimed a glance at Laurence that was equal parts reproach and exasperation. "I was *not* an egg," he said to Laurence. "I was fully grown. We all were."

"Physically," said Laurence, and turned to Patrick. "My young friend, will you please sanitize your hands and then get me those scissors over there? If we can't shave, we at least need to trim. All his fur is making it impossible to close the stitch."

74

"But how? How did you get here?" asked Patrick, pulling up his sleeves and lathering his hands with sanitizer. "Was it a transubstantiation? Like, between Earth and Ith?"

"Well, like I said," continued My-Chale, "none of us remembers enough about our time on Mindth to be able to say exactly what happened. Some old stories have it that one of us is born to a sense world whenever something truly joyous or tragic transpires on one of the two sense worlds. Some event— sometimes just a sound, or image—that focuses the attention of Mindth."

Laurence recited:

"Heat up water and you get steam;
Freeze sound & sight and build a dream."

"So, then, why aren't there any of you on Earth?" asked Patrick, handing Laurence the surgical scissors. "I mean, there are plenty of bad, and sometimes good, things happening, too."

"Well," said My-Chale, "Rex probably best knows the answer to that question, but our best guess is that Earth's tragedies have become so overwhelming that Mindth has turned away and simply stopped listening to what is happening there. Tell me, are there wars?"

"Not near where I live," said Patrick. "But yes. In places like Syria."

"And are people starving?" asked My-Chale.

"In Africa and the Middle East, I think so," said Patrick. "At least sometimes."

"And how many people are living there now?"

"On Earth? About seven billion, you said, right?" said Oma. Patrick nodded.

"Seven billion," said My-Chale. "Yes, that could be a little overwhelming."

Laurence paused and commented, "Seven *billion*!? It would take more than a century to even *count* that high!"

"Wars, famine, and a population so large it staggers the mind," said My-Chale. "You see, we think this is why we are no longer being born on Earth. Rex has simply overwhelmed Mindth's consciousness."

"You mean the Minder?" asked Patrick.

"There is no Minder," said My-Chale.

"But I've heard people say—" said Patrick.

"Yes," said My-Chale. "People like to believe there is one. But, as with many public relations ploys, it's all just a trick to keep people from thinking things through. It's almost always easier for us to imagine a single person is in charge of shaping the world around us."

"Otherwise," Laurence quipped, "personal responsibility might take root and penetrate our laziness and indifference."

"But there is a Seer here on Ith, right?" said Patrick.

"The Minder, the Hearer, the Seer," said My-Chale, "they are fictions concocted by Rex's public relations people. The myth of leadership has always been a highly effective way to manage people, especially scared people. Yes, there is a person, an actual administrator, called the Seer. But she's just a minion, a figurehead, a puppet. Absent Rex, the Deacons are the ones really overseeing the show."

"Okay," said Laurence, snipping a piece of leftover thread. "I did the best I could, but you're probably going to suffer some ingrown hairs. My goodness, you're a big giant furball. At least where you're not feathery and scaly. We should be able to pull out these sutures in a few days.

"Here, Patrick," he continued, "will you please put the scissors back where . . ." His voice trailed off.

Patrick reached out and took the scissors absentmindedly. He was still trying to digest all this stuff about Mindth and the three worlds.

"*What* are those letters on your arm, may I ask?" Laurence interrupted him.

"What? Oh," replied Patrick. "It's a burn I got right before I came to Ith. I bumped against this hot pipe."

"Tell us what it says," Oma told him.

"Well, it reads *ya-way*, I guess."

"Oh. My," said Laurence, and My-Chale made a deep purring sound.

"What?" asked Patrick.

"It sounds like a very old expression," said Laurence. "One of the oldest in all *The Commonplace Book*."

"*Ya-way?*" asked Patrick.

"It means different things to different people," said My-Chale, "but there are common threads to most all of its meanings. Threads that have to do, essentially, with *being*."

"Huh," said Patrick, not really following what they were saying and still curious about Mindth. "Has anybody from Earth or Ith ever gone to Mindth and come back?"

"Well, we all have," replied My-Chale. "We all *do*. It's just the remembering that keeps most of us from being able to say anything about it."

"You're talking about dreams," said Oma.

"Yes," said My-Chale, "for the most part, at least. And artists, musicians, writers, scientists, mathematicians, tinkerers— people who are especially engaged with their dream lives—can even bring elements of the Minders' wisdom into the sense worlds—to Earth and Ith."

"But, wait," said Patrick. "You said, 'for the most part,' about dreams. Do you mean some people actually have *gone* to Mindth?"

"And some have even come back, at least as legend and several religions have it."

"Ith religions?" asked Patrick.

"And Earth," said My-Chale. "You've heard of Nirvana, Elysium, Heaven?"

"Mindth is where we go when we die," said Oma, "right?"

"Not exactly," replied the griffin. "Although Rex and certain other gatekeepers through the ages have liked people to believe that."

"Why?" asked Patrick.

"An afterlife is essentially a second life, yes? One that none of us knows anything about since we've never experienced it ourselves."

"Unless somebody who has been there tells us about it," said Oma.

"Exactly," said My-Chale. "And provided they're not lying."

"Why would anybody lie about that?"

"If you have a test at school and you hear that, if you do badly, you won't get dinner, but if you do well, you'll get dinner and also a huge delicious cake for dessert—will you study harder for the test, or will you do a worse job? Or even think of skipping the test altogether?"

"They make stuff up to convince people to work harder," said Oma.

"Or at least to be obedient and sit quietly in their chairs," said My-Chale.

"The sun's about to set," said Laurence, "and the Reamers will be looking for their killer robot soon. Let's make tracks."

"Agreed," said My-Chale. "Let's get moving. And, Laurence, you can take care of sanitizing this place so they won't find evidence of our stay? And you have another hideout you can make it to by sunrise?"

"Yes, and yes," said Laurence, sounding a bit emotional. "Now, get going. It was a pleasure meeting you, Oma and Patrick."

"Thanks for everything, Laurence," said Oma.

"Yes, thanks, Laurence," said Patrick.

"You're welcome," said the glowing cloud, his eyeholes glistening.

CHAPTER 16

The Quick & the Unconscious

BUNBUN LEAPT JUST IN TIME. THE DRONE'S DARTS penetrated the unkempt grass with a sound like a stomping foot. It seemed to have fired all its ammo, but he wasn't free of it yet. It buzzed back and forth like an enraged hornet.

He thought quickly. The machine was fast and maneuverable. If he ran, it would doubtless catch him from behind.

"Three, two, one," BunBun counted under his breath as the machine plunged. Timing it just right, he jumped and delivered a massive kick that drove the machine straight into the ground. The little drone's fan blades made a noise like an unbalanced Weedwacker and sputtered to a stop.

His foot hurt like crazy, but he didn't think he'd broken it. Before he could examine the bruise, however, there was a loud thump.

"Oh dear," said Mr. BunBun.

A man in a blue electrician's jumpsuit leapt the two-meter vault wall and landed on the ground directly ahead of him.

"Hello, Anarchist," said the man, leveling a pistol-shaped device.

"N-now," said BunBun. "Just because somebody doesn't believe in *your* laws, that doesn't make them an Anarchist."

"Get down on the ground and put your arms behind your back," said the man.

"That's not one of those shocker things, is it?" asked BunBun as he obediently placed his forelegs behind his back.

"This?" asked the man, looking down at the high-tech weapon in his hand. "No, it's a bit more fun than that. It's a dart gun, loaded with just enough neurotoxin to leave you paralyzed and alive so I can take you back to headquarters for some—"

BunBun had many times in books observed the success of the old distract-your-enemy-with-discussion-of-their-superior-equipment-or-skills gambit, but it was the first time he'd ever attempted it himself, in real life. He gave the ground a mighty kick, sending a blast of grass, pebbles, and dirt into the bad man's face.

The weapon discharged, but the venomous barbs plinked harmlessly into the vault wall. BunBun launched himself on a steeply arced, four-meter-high leap that brought him down upon the head and shoulders of his half-blind attacker. The man sprawled to the ground, distinctly unconscious.

"Umm," said BunBun, breathing heavily as he stood over his assailant. He could smell the machinery inside the man. Implants. Nanomechanically enhanced musculature. Neurosilicon circuits. He gently raised one of the man's eyelids and observed the delicate tracery of his ocular screens.

It was just as My-Chale and the others had surmised—when it came to himself and his most trusted servants, Rex did not follow his precious Twelve Tenets (which, among other things, prohibited genetic and surgical modifications). This man was part human, part machine—an enhanced killing and fighting machine.

"Maybe it is *you* who is the enemy of humanity!" BunBun said, finding the man's pulse. BunBun hated the idea of killing anybody.

BunBun then searched the pockets of the man's Kingaroo jumpsuit and found a set of car keys, a binky, and plastic cuffs that had no doubt been meant for him. After tossing the binky to the ground and stomping it to bits, he bound the agent's legs and arms with the plastic cuffs. It didn't seem like the fellow would wake up anytime soon, but there was no sense taking risks.

Other agents would be racing to the scene, so he needed to get moving, and quickly. He left one of his business cards on the man's forehead. This one read:

SOME CAUSE HAPPINESS WHEREVER THEY GO;
OTHERS, WHENEVER THEY GO.
—Oscar Wilde, **BCP §66669143**

He examined the car keys and, recalling the green van he'd seen from the ridge, hurried back up and over the hill.

He took great care not to be seen, but as he bounded out of the trees and across the sidewalk, he noticed a woman at the third-floor window of the apartment building across the street. When she saw him, she stopped washing her dishes in the sink and dropped her mouth open.

BunBun figured there was no chance of her unseeing him, so he stopped, smiled, and gave a sheepish wave.

The woman closed her mouth, and for a moment it looked like she was about to wave back. Instead she scowled, turned off the faucet, left whatever she'd been washing in the sink, rubbed her eyes, turned, and stalked back into the depths of her apartment.

As he unlocked the passenger-side door and climbed into the van, it occurred to him he was a little disappointed she hadn't been more friendly, but at the same time, it had obviously been a good thing she hadn't taken his picture or screamed her head off or anything like that.

It was a good thing, too, that when he'd still had his binky and had been waiting around in Hedgerow Heights, he'd gotten curious about all the cars and trucks he'd seen going by on the surrounding roads, and had done a little research about how they were operated.

Still, reading about how to do something and actually doing it are two very different things. And the owner's manual wasn't exactly set up like a how-to book. But before long he did manage to turn on the engine, and then determine which was the brake pedal and which the accelerator.

The hardest part was navigating something so much bigger than he was, but—after a halting, tentative start that caused the vehicles behind him to make loud honking noises— he pretty much got the hang of the thing.

And so he made it several miles—almost to the Broadway Bridge connecting the Bronx with Manhattan over the Harlem River—before crashing.

CHAPTER 17
Invisibilus Rex

WHAT'S GOING ON, ANDREW?" ASKED RICK Griffin. "We didn't miss the message that you'd be coming to town, did we?" His brother-in-law, a research chemist for the government in Washington, DC, looked like he hadn't slept in days. If he had, he'd clearly done it in the same rumpled clothes he was now wearing.

"Just happened to be in the area," Andrew replied.

When he was done hugging all the children and had finished passing out licorice (even for Lucie and Neil), he turned to Rick and Mary.

"Someplace we can talk in private?" he asked.

"Sure, let's go in the TV room," said Rick.

Mary told the kids to go make themselves breakfast, and the three grownups crossed the living room and slid closed the den doors behind them.

"Turn off your cell phone, please," Andrew said to his sister. She did so and he continued, "The voice-activated software keeps the microphone switched on and—under the guise of listening for 'command' words—anybody could be listening, recording, transmitting any conversation in range. You don't have one of those camera or microphone controllers for the game console in here, do you, Rick? I don't see one."

"We do, but it's unplugged. Creeps me out having a company able to look into my home."

"And it should," replied Andrew.

"Andrew?" said Mary, looking at her brother with concern.

"So," said Rick, "what's with arriving unannounced like this, looking like you've been living out of your car—"

"I am a little unpresentable, aren't I?" his brother-in-law replied, feeling the short brown stubble on his chin. "I haven't been sleeping much since Patrick went missing."

The Griffin children's uncle started to cry. In a moment, all three adults were sobbing.

"I wish I knew what was going on," Andrew finally managed. "Suffice it to say something *very* strange is going on in connection with Patrick's disappearance. Did I hear he called you Monday morning?"

"Yes," said Rick. "Basically he told us he was okay and he warned us to be careful, and not to talk to people about the fact that he called. It's crazy-sounding I know, but he really did seem okay when he called. It's the one aspect of this whole insane situation that gives us any comfort. He mentioned some man—"

"Rex Abraham!?" asked Andrew.

"Yeah, that was the name," said Rick.

Andrew put his hands on his head as if to keep his skull together. "You're positive that was the name?"

"Definitely," replied Rick.

"Okay," said Andrew, nodding his balding, unkempt head. "You ever hear of him?"

Rick and Mary shook their heads.

"There have been and remain more than one Rex Abraham in the world. But I'm pretty sure Patrick was referring to the one who was a pioneering electrical engineer during the sixties, a defense contractor during the Vietnam War, a systems engineer in California in the late seventies, a patent-winning researcher at an optics laboratory in New Jersey in the eighties, a wireless data systems planner in the nineties and, since then, he's had board positions everyplace from Xerox to Raytheon to IBM to General Dynamics to Microsoft to Apple. Most recently, he was the founder of a modern telecom corporation called Kingaroo—"

"Kingaroo?" said Rick. "They made the home router package I bought so we can adjust the thermostat, check the locks, set the alarm system remotely—"

"Same company, yes," said Andrew. "Great price, right?"

"It was pretty cheap," admitted Rick.

"That's because Kingaroo isn't in business to make money."

"What are they in business for?" asked Mary.

"They're in business to do whatever Rex wants. Or, at least, wanted to do. When he still existed."

"What do you mean?" said Mary. "He's dead?"

"He's gone," said Andrew. "He was never quite front-page-news famous, never listed as a fat cat in Forbes, never did any TED Talks or consumer electronics presentations—he was kind of famous for being anonymous. The Thomas Pynchon of the tech industry. And then, suddenly, in just the past few days, he disappeared."

"Like," said Mary, "dropped out of the public eye?"

"Like he dropped out of the public *brain*. His Wikipedia entry, his company bio at Kingaroo, his mention in old news stories, even his listing in *government databases* is no longer there."

"What do you mean?" asked Mary.

"I have a good college friend in the DNPA—the Data Network Protection Administration. Remember Zippy Metcalf, Mary?"

"With the glasses and the ski sweaters?"

Andrew nodded. "Anyhow, when I got Patrick's message, I asked Zippy to trace the call. It originated in France."

"Yes, he said he was in France," observed Rick.

"We've been talking about going there to look for him," said Mary.

"I don't think he's there any longer," said Andrew. "Bear with me here. So, anyhow, as Zippy was pulling the call records, the traces suddenly disappeared. Poof. Just gone. So he and some colleagues looked into it—how could public phone records just disappear like that?—and nobody has any idea. But they did find out one interesting thing. The call was routed through servers managed by . . . any guesses?"

"Kingaroo," said Mary.

"Bingo. So clearly somebody on their end just wiped out the data. Which of course led me to start finding out more about this company. I knew they were into networking protocols and device manufacture—some real high-end stuff—but I had no idea they handled, at least directly, cell-phone traffic.

"And then the coincidences really started piling up. On Monday Kingaroo suddenly announced a drug company acquisition—which is bizarre, because they're data, not pharmaceutical. So my curiosity was piqued, and I started to google him, and, well, there wasn't a trace of him."

"Are you sure," said Mary, "that you and Zippy had the right name?"

"Yes. I mean, Zippy and I weren't the only ones to know his name. We talked to at least a dozen colleagues who'd heard of him and none of us could find *anything* about him. Not even in government files. So, as things stand, this Rex Abraham— scientist, researcher, investor, businessman—never existed."

"But the government," Rick asked, "aren't they looking into it? Isn't that a big deal if a taxpayer suddenly disappears?"

"Yeah, they started to. Zippy called a guy he knows over at the FBI and they started a case but it got shut down in a matter of hours. This memo came down basically saying Rex was never a real person. It had all been an elaborate prank."

"Weird," said Rick.

"And even weirder is if it was a prank, then how come

there was no Wikipedia entry or anything *anywhere* on the Internet about it?"

"Makes you wish we had good old-fashioned books and newspapers," said Rick. "You can't go into somebody's house and erase what's written on paper!"

"That occurred to me," said Andrew. "Tuesday I went down to the Library of Congress to check out some bound corporate listings from companies where I remembered reading that Rex had worked and, you know what? The corporate records wing was getting refurbished and they couldn't get the volumes for me."

"That's a weird coincidence," said Mary.

"Or something," said Rick.

"So," said Andrew, "either I and everybody who has heard of Rex are suffering from a mass-hallucinatory memory, or somebody has taken great pains to get Rex's name scrubbed from the public record. If you were to google his name right now—which, please don't, I'll tell you why shortly—you'd see no sign of the guy I'm talking about."

"So what does it mean?" asked Rick.

"It means," said Andrew, "that Patrick knows something of what's going on. And that this Rex guy is somehow involved. So, besides telling you to keep your ears and eyes alert, I bet Patrick told you not to tell anybody he'd spoken to you, right? That it could be dangerous to the family?"

"Yes," replied Rick.

"And he was right," said Andrew. "That's why I came here in person to talk, rather than calling or e-mailing about it. Whoever erased Rex's name from the public record, from the

Internet, is very concerned about *not* attracting attention to whatever's going on here. It's almost like they knew Patrick or somebody he's with had stumbled onto something about Rex and decided to cover their tracks. But the scary thing is, if somebody like Rex can disappear like that, think what can happen to regular people like us."

"But it doesn't make any sense," said Mary. "Why would a seventh-grade boy be mixed up in some sort of corporate conspiracy?"

"That, I don't have a clue about," said Andrew. "Except that sometimes accidents happen. He spends some time on the computer, right? Maybe he found something he shouldn't have seen."

"Well, the police searched all the computers in the house, and all our social media accounts, and they didn't find anything," said Mary.

"If the founder of the company that made your home's wireless network hardware has disappeared," asked Andrew, "do you think it's possible such a search might be flawed?"

Mary nodded, her lip quivering all of a sudden.

"Patrick definitely seemed to be trying to warn us about something," said Rick.

"What else did he say?" asked Andrew.

"Tell him, Rick," said Mary, and Rick told him how Patrick had mentioned terrorists, and had told them to get gas masks.

Andrew rubbed his stubbled chin again and nodded. "Anything else?"

"Well, this is especially weird . . ." Rick looked to his wife again before continuing. "He told me to ask the Twins if they'd seen a big talking rabbit."

"And had they?" asked Andrew.

"Yes," said Rick. "They've been talking about a big talking rabbit for days. Of course they also routinely converse with imaginary talking giant sloths and triceratops—they're four years old."

"What are you thinking, Andrew? Does any of what Patrick said actually make sense?"

"Too much sense," said Andrew.

"Not about the rabbit, though," said Rick. "That was Patrick just being nice, right? We figured he was just being a good brother, sending them his best wishes in a way they'd appreciate?"

"Well, I'd almost think so, except get this: I received an encrypted message on my personal e-mail. The message told me to stop searching about Rex Abraham online, to watch out for all people with first names for last names, and, for my own safety, to delete the voice mail from Patrick."

"Who was it from?" asked Mary.

"It was signed, get this, *Mr. BunBun.*"

At this moment there was a hubbub out in the hallway—it sounded like the children were fighting. A moment later the door to the den slid open and Carly came into the room, followed by Neil, Lucie, and the rest of the Griffin children.

"Mom, Neil was spying on you guys!" said Carly.

"It's true," said Neil. "And we know all about Mr. Bun-Bun, too. We *met* him."

CHAPTER 18
Progress Reports

BACK IN HIS COMPOUND ON THE OUTSKIRTS OF Silicon City, Rex caught up on Ith's past forty years. He was generally pleased with the progress.

The population had been well managed. The vestiges of the messy, inefficient old world had been largely erased, and the wide-eyed, peace-loving new population was being raised in a world of unprecedented order and harmony. The hyper-efficient economy kept goods and services flowing without interruption, and virtual reality entertainments were so realistic and compelling that people no longer needed to leave their homes to feel they'd left their homes—vacation travel was a thing of the past. And, on top of all that, robotic domestic servants had nearly eliminated personal labor, and the natural world—not that many citizens went outside to experience it—had been cleansed of all nuisance and nonessential species. There were now no mosquitoes, blackflies, horseflies, chiggers, fire ants, ticks, man-eating sharks, venomous snakes, rats, mice, raccoons, skunks, poison ivy, stinging nettles, or leeches on Ith. Never in history had a human population been more content.

And now the government was at work on projects to stabilize the weather and the very geology of the planet. Cooling towers and solar convection lenses were reducing the prevalence of severe storms, and geothermal stasis-taps had begun to lessen tectonic drift and the risk of disastrous earthquakes, tsunamis, and volcanic eruptions. In a matter of another three decades, such economically disruptive phenomena would be entirely eliminated.

And if he needed further proof of his success, there was only one factor that need be considered: *not a single new Mindthling had been sent to Ith since his departure.*

There were a few still alive here, of course. Not only had it been something of a test—he'd wanted to prove that his system could withstand their anarchic influence—but he needed the transcense. The key ingredient of transubstantiation didn't last long, and the only way to get more was to harvest it from recently deceased Mindthlings. He'd just killed the second-to-last Mindthling on Earth (a white-haired yeti in the Himalayas) to make this trip to Ith.

It wasn't an ideal situation, but until his scientists figured out how to synthesize the transcense from scratch, it was just how things were.

Also in the less-than-ideal category was the boy, the boy from Earth. The one who went to Ith and back to Earth and back to Ith again. The Griffin boy. He scowled as he considered the coincidence of the boy's name and the chimeric leader of the Mindthling resistance.

He accepted a smoothie from a serving robot and commanded the windows of his seaside home to shut out the daylight as he took a seat in his Otto Williams chair and processed an executive brief entitled,

patrik grifin: wᴀʀabɒts unnōn, sᴜʀc ongōing

The boy had been brainwashed by the Mindthlings and, even as hopeless as their cause was, this had not been anticipated and therefore was not a good thing.

He initiated another holo-call to the Seer.

"Your Awarenence," said the nervous woman's image, nodding like a dashboard bobblehead.

Rex sighed. He maybe should have contacted the Deacons directly. The Seer was such a clueless little toady. But he wanted to keep the Deacons on edge. They'd had a relatively easy time of it without him here these past forty years, or "yies" as they were known here on Ith. They had doubtless become a little soft, a little overconfident.

Also, though the Seer had aged rather dramatically (the decades had added more than crows' feet to the face of Ith's oldest human being), he still preferred having his eyes upon her as opposed to any of Ith's twelve disfigured Deacons.

"Tell Karen Grace and William George at YSS that I wish to

visit the Mindthling camp. I'll want a research update as well as at least two interrogation sessions.

"And tell Matthew Roy and Simon Stewart at POP that I want a full report on the status of the search for the Earth boy. It is the *height* of incompetence that he remains missing."

"Yes, of course, Your Awarenence," she said, her head bobbling back and forth even more rapidly than usual. He selected an icon on his retinal display, and Ith's temperature-regulated, sharkless, jellyfishless Pacific Ocean appeared through the windows once again. Perhaps he'd go down for a quick swim before his inspection visit.

CHAPTER 19

Once Upon a Pawn

KEMPTON PUBER, OMA'S LITTLE BROTHER, SLEW another dragon—this time with a rail-gun shot right through its ugly Class III lizard head—and thought to himself how lucky it was that the newest version of the video game Abomination Redress Squad 6D had come out this week. The ARS game franchise was the most popular home game on Ith for boys seven and up. Without it, he was sure he would have needed double counseling sessions.

Since the enormous Class II had smashed open their house and taken Patrick Griffin away, the Pubers' lives had been completely upside down.

The temporary facility they had been placed in while their

home was repaired was a big part of it. The screen-tech in the place was at least four generations old, his bed didn't have an active-response mattress, the serving bots were so slow you almost might as well go get the food from the kitchen yourself, and the gaming chair was utterly substandard and couldn't even do a barrel roll.

And then there had been the nasty, really awful way in which the ARS investigators had treated them. It was almost as if they thought Kempton and his parents *had something to do with* his sister and Patrick Griffin's abduction. Why had their perimeter security system not worked? (The storm—the biggest in nearly a decade—had apparently overwhelmed the grid.) Why hadn't Kempton and the parents immediately messaged for help when the abomination attacked the house? (They had wanted to but, again, the grid was blacked out.) What sort of friends did Oma keep at school, and had she behaved strangely in the past few months? (Oma was no stranger than any teenage girl, said Mr. and Mrs. Puber, although Kempton, in a private interview later, would admit that she'd been strange all her life—a loner, and sometimes sarcastic about school and government.)

There was definitely an imputation that he and his parents were, if not complicit, at least negligent. Which was ridiculous. His father was a stickler for security and safety. Dad had run two fire drills for the family just last week, once interrupting dinner to have the family assemble at the nearest Community Safe Point, and his mother compulsively made Kempton and Oma read every POP (Public Operations Panel) bulletin ever issued.

And Kempton, for his part, had been school Echelon Safety Warden three years running and had earned over eighty-three citizenry credits—the third-highest total in his age bracket.

The interrogation had been entirely demoralizing, and not just to Kempton. His father had been having trouble sleeping and had taken to muttering under his breath all day long. His mother broke into tears every time she looked up from her binky.

The two of them were way more upset about Oma's disappearance than he was. As far as he was concerned, Oma deserved nothing but resentment. Her dubious life choices—the school uniform violations, the substandard academic scores, the subversive things she sometimes said about their academic and municipal admins—had always been annoying. But now, with the investigators trying to make sense of Patrick Griffin's and her disappearance, the entire family's reputation was in jeopardy.

Although the gaming room at their temporary housing was a generation and a half out-of-date, he had been taking out most of his aggressions in it. Since the last interview, he'd spent four of the past five hours strapped in its dated gaming chair.

"SR-Sitzen, D-Con Soldja!" he addressed his virtual game-mates. "Flank me—I'm going for the main base!"

"You need to level up before you try that, ABK-96!" responded an adolescent voice. "There's no way you have the shield points."

"Yeah, they'll fry you like a quinoa fritter," said another boy's voice.

"Maybe you little wusses should have your mothers come bring you a snack and a—" he was replying when the game shut off.

"What a piece of feces!" said Kempton, clambering angrily out of the game chair and giving it a swift kick. "When are we going to get to move back to a place with halfway decent—"

A bright orange communications orb, marked with the logo of the Ministry of Communications

appeared in the middle of the room just then along with a message:

inkuming koʟʟ : prɪorɘtᴇ ʟᴇvɘl 1

"Priority level one?" said Kempton, dumbfounded. "Here? For me?" Level one meant Deacon!

He quickly selected the answer icon, and a young woman with a high collar and reflective eye shadow appeared in holograph.

"Kempton Puber," she said, "I am a personal coordinator for Sabrina Kim of the Ministry of Communications."

"Oh," said Kempton. "Yes, yes, wow, yes," he said, nodding like a 1950s TV child star. "It is an honor—"

"She has a task she'd like you to undertake on behalf of the Ministry of Communications. A transport will arrive at your place of residence in three deuces. Please bring at least one change of clothes and your personal hygiene items. We may need to keep you overnight in Silicon City."

"Oh," said Kempton, nearly too excited to speak. "Of course."

The communication stopped and Kempton ran from the room screaming—in a happy way—for his mother.

PART II: PRIMATES

If you bring forth what is inside you, what you bring
forth will save you. If you don't bring forth what is inside you, what you bring forth will destroy you.

—*The Gnostic Gospel of Thomas*
bcp §4¶8

CHAPTER 20
Northwest Air

EVEN WITH THE EXTRA BLANKETS, IT WAS SO COLD
that Oma and Patrick promised not to talk about it anymore. As if, by changing the topic, they could distract themselves from it.

Huddling as close together as they could, both to keep warm and to be able to hear each other over the rushing roar of My-Chale's powerful wing-strokes, Oma and Patrick had embarked on what, to Patrick, was one of the most meaningful, memorable conversations he had ever had with anybody.

They spoke of missing their families. They spoke of being nevertheless certain they were doing the right thing. They spoke of the things they'd learned that most blew their minds.

Patrick especially couldn't get over the fact that Earth had once had Mindthlings—creatures like Laurence, My-Chale, and Purse-Phone, the giant who had taken them away from the Pubers' house. It made some level of sense. There were lots of monsters in old legends. The Greeks and Romans had Cyclopes and Minotaurs. Europe and Asia had dragons, unicorns, and trolls. The Americas had giants, thunderbirds, and winged serpents. It seemed maybe there had been a kernel of truth to at least some of them.

Oma was fascinated to hear Patrick talking about how things were on Earth. She was curious about how Patrick's home world could have so many people on it—billions of them. Ith had mere millions. She told Patrick that Rex and the Deacons had long ago settled on an ideal population level, preventing people from having more than two children, and keeping inhabited areas in strictly controlled parts of the planet.

Which obviously didn't include the territory they were now overflying. The land below was as dark as the backside of the moon. No twinkling lights like Patrick had seen out a nighttime airplane window back on Earth. Just blackness and the occasional eerie reflection of moon or stars on a lake or river.

Toward morning, as the sky began to glow pink behind them, they descended through the Snoqualmie Pass and saw their destination for the first time: the derelict skyline of Seattle. The Space Needle—minus its antenna mast—was still standing, as was a small crowd of rectangular office buildings, ghostly, jagged-peaked, the sky behind them showing through the missing windows and interior walls.

Off to the right, a small bright light began pulsing from a hill behind the Space Needle.

"Morse code," said My-Chale. "It says, let's see, that's *W*, that's *O* . . . that's *A*, I think . . . and dah-dit-dit I think is *D* . . . so, hang on . . . and it's starting over now. Okay, the message is, 'I wasted time, and now doth time waste me.' "

"What does *that* mean?" said Oma.

"Shakespeare, I think," said My-Chale. "It's about getting old and having wasted chances to do things when you're young. Section seven of *The Commonplace*."

"Why would somebody be Morse-coding us that?" asked Patrick.

"That's just Ivan letting me know it's him," replied the griffin as he dove toward the light.

CHAPTER 21

Over the Side

BUNBUN HAD TRIED TO NAVIGATE THE VEHICLE across the busy intersection, but an aggressive yellow car with a colorful plastic cap and little lights on its roof had rattled his attention, pulling a handsbreadth behind him and honking repeatedly. He'd meant to hit the brake pedal but had instead stomped the accelerator, quickly losing control of the van and crashing it into the steel support for the elevated train. Through the broken windshield, somebody had yelled, "You idiot—that was a red light!"

"Which one?" BunBun had groaned. As far as he could tell, there were more than a million red lights in this crazy city— on sign posts, in windows, in the back windshields of cars, and flashing on the fenders of bicycles. And there were green and yellow and blue and strobing white ones, too—a firestorm of visual insanity. He was frankly amazed that his was the first accident he'd seen.

"You ought to have your license revoked!" somebody shouted as he pushed down the airbag and kicked open the somewhat stuck driver's door.

The same voice said, "What the—!?" as BunBun leapt out onto the busy street.

Another yelled, "Yo, Easter Bunny, wrong holiday! It's St. Paddy's Day!"

"What are you supposed to be?!" yelled another. "A jacka-lope?!"

The sound of approaching sirens plus the fear of having his picture taken kept him from replying. He bounded as fast as he could—a good deal faster than the traffic—onto the Broadway Bridge, and had made it halfway across when he saw flashing lights and heard a wobbly, electric siren blaring from the opposite side.

"Oh no, oh no," he said as he saw a man getting out of his car and aiming a smartphone at him.

Almost without hesitation (he did take a quick look over the railing first, just to make sure he wasn't going to land on something hard and/or pointy), he leapt over the side, and plunged into the salty, chilly, murky depths of the Harlem River.

CHAPTER 22
Heated Frays & Train Delays

AS THE NUMBATS PELL-MELLED TOWARD THE BACK of the commuter train, most of the human passengers cowered or ran the opposite way. Unfortunately, there were some exceptions.

A terrifying number of umbrellas, shoes, and briefcases were swung, stomped, or thrown in their general direction.

"Hurry up!" Sven kept shouting. And, "This way!"

As if, Barb thought, running for their lives in a straight line could be done with greater urgency or direction.

"Any ideas, Trixy?" asked Shifty. Her sister was examining the last car's firmly locked rear door. The railroad naturally had no interest in people accidentally stepping off the back-side of a speeding train.

Trixy was the most mechanically gifted of the Nine, but she was no miracle worker.

"We're doomed!" said Shorty, not very helpfully.

"These people are giving me a headache," said Tenty, glaring back up the train car. "Can't they knock off the yelling? I swear—if one more person calls us rats!"

"One man said we were coatimundis," said Shifty.

"Well, that's just about the stupidest thing ever said," said Barb. "Do I have a striped tail and basically resemble a banana-headed tropical raccoon?"

"Uh-oh," said Levanty, and gave a terrific sneeze. "These two look like trouble."

Most of the car had cleared out by now, but two young men in security guard uniforms, doubtless on their way to work, were making their way down the aisle. Each brandished a black enameled nightstick.

"What do you think they are, Frank?" asked one of the men, the guy with the shorter crewcut.

"I think they're lemurs," said the other—Frank, apparently—with the amber-tinted glasses.

"Bull," said the first. "Lemurs don't have pointy noses like that—they're some kind of baby anteaters or something."

"Whatchamacallit? Aardvarks?"

"I think aardvarks are bigger."

"Aw, maybe they're *baby* aardvarks," said Frank.

Barb was fit to be tied. The very idea of them being baby

aardvarks was so incredibly stupid it hurt her brain to even consider.

"You know," said the first security guard, "I'm pretty sure aardvarks have less-pointy noses than that. Kind of like beer cans, you know? Only, you know, soft, furry beer cans. With whatchamacall'em—those nose-holes in the end."

"Nostrils," said the second man.

"And to think I was expecting Earth humans to be smarter than the Ith ones," whispered Barb.

"Shhh," whispered Sven. "Remember, no talkie—we stupid *animals*!"

The first man paused and said, "Right, nostrils."

"You know," said the second man, "I don't think I've ever seen aardvarks up this close."

"They're not aardvarks," said the first. "Aardvarks have wrinkly gray skin, you know, like little elephants."

"Nuh-uh," said the other. "I saw one on TV and it had fur."

"Well, you saw something on TV, but I saw an *aardvark* at the zoo, and he was gray and wrinkly just like a little elephant."

"You sure that was a zoo you were at, Frank—not a family reunion or something?"

"Yeah, maybe *your* family reunion," said the one named Frank.

"All right, all right. You know, I actually think these guys might be from Australia. I think they're called wombats or something."

Barb snarled and Sven shot her a reproachful glance.

"That one there looks angry," said the second man.

112

"Aren't *you* a snarly little wombat," said the first.

Barb had no trouble summoning another snarl in reply.

"If they don't have rabies and we take them home as pets, you get that one. Looks like a biter."

"Hey, what are we doing not taking pictures of these guys, anyway?" said Frank, reaching for his smartphone. "This'll be huge on my Instagram."

Fortunately, before either of the men could get out his smartphone, a passenger in a forward car pulled the emergency brake cord and the train's wheels locked, sending the numbats—and the two security guards—rolling down into a heap at the front end of the car.

"Aaaaah!" screamed both men as they swung madly about themselves with their nightsticks.

"One of them bit me!" shouted one, which wasn't true—he'd been pinched by one of the equipment clips on his friend's corded belt.

"Aim for their heads," said the one named Frank, flailing about himself.

The Nine quickly extricated themselves from the scrum and sprinted back up the aisle.

All but Shifty, the reader of the group, were soon at the rear end of the car. Shifty had become fascinated with a piece of Earth writing below one of the passenger windows.

She entered the row of seats to the left and clambered up on the vinyl-upholstered bench. "This says 'Emergency Exit'!" she yelled. "Here, come give me a hand, you guys!"

She sounded out the rest of the words she saw written on the white decal underneath the window, "Pull red . . . hand . . .

le—handle! . . . and rem-oh-veh—that must be remove!—
gas-ket, pusss-huh—*push!*—glass . . . *outward!"*

And so the Nine quickly removed the black rubber seal
around the emergency rescue window and pushed it out onto
the gravel bed next to the motionless train. Then it was a simple
matter of forming a human—or, rather, a numbat—chain and
clambering out onto the rail bed.

And then disappearing into the greening thickets along
the southern bank of the Anacostia River.

CHAPTER 23
Genius Meat

THE FLASHING LIGHT WAS COMING FROM A BIG blocky stone building near the top of the hill. It looked to Patrick like a big old-fashioned school and, as My-Chale landed in the overgrown courtyard, the still-legible letters above the moss-covered entryway—*QUEEN ANNE HIGH SCHOOL*—proved him right.

"He's probably waiting for us inside," said My-Chale as Oma and Patrick slid off his back.

They regarded the crumbling, vegetation-covered structure in front of them. Long ago its front doors had been taken off their hinges. The interior was a tide pool of inky gloom in the predawn light.

"Not too inviting," said Patrick.

"Forty years of neglect will do that to a place," said My-Chale.

"You sure he's here?" asked Oma.

"Probably busy in his lab."

"Hey, look, a Commonplace marker," said Oma, her big eyes picking out a message written in chalk upon the dirty old steps.

. . . genius is so much meat in motion.
—Natalie Angier BCP§549144

"Well, *that's* a weird one," said Patrick.

"Yes," said My-Chale. "That's Ivan all right. He has a thing against exceptionalism."

"What's that?" asked Patrick.

"Exceptionalism? A belief that certain individuals are significantly better than others and that different rules should apply to them."

"Like, you mean, geniuses?" asked Patrick.

"Yes," said a sarcasm-dripping voice from an upstairs window, "like what you are *not*, standing out there as the sun is about to come up in a sky that is filled with hundreds of high-resolution cameras. Get your butts up to the second floor and see Ivan."

"Hi, Seth!" My-Chale shouted.

"Howdy, My-Chale," replied the voice.

"Go on up, you two," My-Chale said to Oma and Patrick,

untucking his massive wings and backing to the center of the courtyard. "I'll see you in a few days."

"What?" said Oma, surprised.

Patrick felt some misgiving himself. Their fearless leader was leaving them all alone in this strange place?

"You'll be fine," said My-Chale. "Ivan is a good friend, and you'll have ample help for the next part of the mission."

"But where are you going?" asked Patrick.

"I have to pick up a talented friend," said My-Chale. "Really, you'll be fine. That *Commonplace* entry right there makes the point quite well. It's not just that the notion of genius is overplayed, it's that we all need to have the confidence to act against it. We need to take responsibility for kindling *our own* spirits, and to stop waiting for somebody exceptional to do it for us."

The griffin reared up on his hind legs and began to beat his wings. Patrick didn't know whether he or she had initiated it, but he realized he and Oma were holding hands.

"In other words," said My-Chale, "you need to seize the day. You need to realize that *you* can make a difference. And that you do have the tools—even the genius—to do so."

"So," said Patrick, "in other words, believe in ourselves."

Oma laughed.

"Well, *that's* probably not going to make it into *The Book of Commonplace*," said My-Chale. "But, yes, essentially that's it. Don't sit back. Don't wait around for me or for anybody else to do what you know to be right. You are here on this world for a reason. Each of us is.

"Now," he said, somehow smiling despite having no lips, "be good."

Patrick and Oma let go of each other's hand so that they could cover their faces against the blast of dust and dead leaves My-Chale's wings kicked up as he leapt into the sky.

CHAPTER 24
Lead Investigator

MARY MEYER GRIFFIN HAD NEVER FELT MORE
certain of herself or her actions. On their own, the facts
in front of her were absolutely bizarre. Her children talking
to a giant antlered rabbit? A tech magnate named Rex Abraham disappearing from the public record? The distinct smell
of church incense in their house immediately after Patrick's
disappearance? Her brother Andrew's corporate-governmental
conspiracy theories? Patrick's call on Monday telling them he
was okay but urging them to get gas masks? Each was too
strange to believe. And yet somehow—all together—it made
clear a pattern.

The police and FBI might be at a loss—they hadn't reported

a single lead since Saturday—but Mary Meyer Griffin wasn't going to sit around waiting for information to come to her.

Her first instinct had been to set up a project using the Basecamp online productivity software she used at work, but of course that would fly in the face of Andrew's cautions about doing anything online. So she and Rick and Andrew brought the chalkboard up from the playroom to the den. And there, and on Post-its and pieces of notebook paper taped to the wall, she had everybody put down (using specific chalk and marker colors) all the facts they knew, and decided where to focus their efforts.

First, she ruled out France. Even though Patrick had apparently called from there, what indication did they have that he'd still be there three days later? And of course they had no idea *where* in France he might have been. Perhaps he'd been in Paris. Perhaps he'd been in the hometown of the woman who'd appeared in Corpus Christi. Perhaps, suggested Eva, he might be in Cannes.

New York City, on the other hand, was too promising—and close—to ignore. First, they had the Twins insisting that the Museum of Natural History was BunBun's destination. Second, they had the older children saying he was intent on appearing on television (which could really happen anywhere, but of course there were a lot of TV stations and news bureaus in the city). Third, they had the creature's recent sighting in Van Cortlandt Park.

And, fourth, as of a little while ago, they had the news feed Neil had spotted about a small man in a rabbit suit crashing a stolen van into the Broadway Bridge, right on the border of the Bronx and Manhattan.

Only Mary had a chance to glimpse the article because even as Neil called everybody over to look, a pop-up advertisement came up and blocked the piece, and then wouldn't close.

Mary wondered if the rabbit—or the man in the rabbit suit—could be a bad guy, could in fact be behind Patrick's disappearance. But what kind of bad guy steals one kid and then pleasantly chats with others and appears to be the only contributor to *any* understanding of what is going on?

They turned off the computer and restarted it, and when Neil searched for the story again, it was nowhere to be found.

"Well, there's some déjà vu," said Uncle Andrew, and asked, pointedly, if they'd noticed what the ad had been for.

"King*aroo*," said Carly ominously.

"Hey," said Neil suddenly. "What time did Patrick call on Monday?"

"About nine in the morning," said Mary.

"And he left a message for me shortly before nine a.m.," said Uncle Andrew.

"And, Ma and Lucie, didn't you say the house smelled like incense the morning Patrick disappeared? You know, while I was at lacrosse?"

"Yes, why, Neil?" asked his mother.

"Because, have you guys seen this? This story has been popping up on the news for the past couple days but I just finally read into it."

The computer headline read, *FRENCH MIRACLE WOMAN STILL REFUSING TO LEAVE TEXAS CHURCH.*

Lilian Carruth, a retired eighty-year-old secondary school language teacher from France, was reported missing from her rural home Monday. Her family claims she had been cooking dinner when there was a small explosion and she was suddenly missing from the premises.

The family and the first police arriving on the scene reported the smell of "church incense" in the house.

The story has been garnering international attention because the woman was found halfway around the world less than one hour after her family reported her missing. Mme. Carruth—wearing slippers and still carrying a spatula—somehow managed to find herself inside a Corpus Christi, Texas, church, forty-eight minutes after her family called 112 (the French equivalent of 911).

A stunt on the part of the family was immediately suspected, but more than fifty eyewitnesses have confirmed seeing Carruth two hours prior at her own church in Mauléon-Licharre, France—clearly still not enough time to travel five thousand miles by any conventional means of transportation. Speculation now is that the incident is a publicity-seeking hoax concocted by the woman's church. Chief religion correspondent for KNS News Gabby Lauren says, "Experts believe it may be a Shroud of Turin–style prank, meant to drum up publicity and dollars.

"Local church officials deny any involvement, and the Vatican has not released any statements about the matter."

Meantime, Carruth has refused to leave the Texas church, and hundreds of pilgrims have begun arriving in Corpus Christi, lining up around the block to get an audience with the French Miracle Woman.

"Corpus Christi," said Neil, "that's where they're taking that giant squid they caught."

"Hey," said Lucie. "France is like five hours ahead of us and Texas is an hour behind us, right? So, doesn't that mean this woman disappeared from France and showed up in Texas right around the time that Patrick was calling?"

"Yes," said Mary, scribbling on the chalkboard. "Patrick calls us right around the time this French woman vanished from her home. Then he hangs up and we hear nothing, and next thing you know this old lady shows up in a Texas church."

"Holy sh—" Neil started to say before his dad whacked him on the back of the head with a rolled-up copy of *Publishers Weekly*.

"Language," said his father.

"I'm just wondering how this all worked," said Mary. "Patrick disappears into thin air and comes back to France two days later and calls us and then disappears again? And a woman in France at the same time ends up in Texas?"

"Maybe Patrick and this lady are sharing a TARDIS," said Neil, referencing the time-travel machine in *Doctor Who*.

"And notice the name of the woman in the article who's saying it's all a hoax," said Andrew. "Gabby Lauren. She has a first name for a last name."

"This is so crazy," said Lucie.

"Unusual circumstances demand unusual explanations," quipped Mary. "And unusual responses."

And here Mrs. Griffin outlined the second part of the game plan: past trying to find this BunBun creature in New York, it was clear the woman in Texas needed to be interviewed. The circumstances around her and Patrick were far too similar to ignore, and though she was farther away, at least—unlike BunBun—they knew exactly where she was.

"Andrew," she said, "how do you feel about taking a trip to Texas?"

"Can I go, too?" said Neil.

"That would be great with me, if it's okay with your parents," said Andrew. "It'll be an adventure."

Mary looked at Rick and her husband shrugged.

"I think that will be fine," she said, and turned to her husband. "Honey, let's use your hotel and air points we were saving for the European trip, don't you think?"

"I don't mind paying for my and Neil's travel," said Andrew. "I have plenty of points myself. Please."

"Really, Andrew?" Mary asked.

"Really," her brother replied.

"Well, in that case, I think it makes sense for us to use Rick's points to get us some hotel rooms in New York," said Mary. "If we can fit four to a room—let's see," she said, counting around the room and then saying, "and Nana—whom I need to call right now and tell her what the plan is—we should be able to fit in three rooms. You can make us reservations online, right, honey?"

"Uh," said Rick, "sure."

"I mean," continued Mary, "who knows if we're going to find BunBun today. And anyhow, it will be good for us to get out of this house."

And so, at Mary's instruction, the rest of the family packed, and Mary's mother, Nana, came over, and by noon, the generally bustling Griffin house was empty for the first in a long stretch of unoccupied days.

CHAPTER 25
Plaudits & Plausibilities

ALONG-BEARDED MAN WEARING A BINKY OVER HIS
eyes and a blue collar around his neck was waiting for
Patrick and Oma in an electronics-filled gymnasium on the
second floor of the abandoned school. He was clapping, but
not—as it turned out—because he was happy about their
arrival.

"Welcome to the . . . PN-Triple-C," he gasped. "The Pacific
Northwest . . . Commonplace Command . . . Center." He had
some sort of breathing issue that kept him from stringing too
many words together. Patrick was reminded of Nana when she
had a cold. Nana smoked cigarettes. A lot of cigarettes.

The man removed the binky from his face, revealing two

bag-saddled eyes, and introduced himself as Ivan Dunn. Then he apologized for clapping. MoK (Motor operative Control) collars, he explained, essentially work by radio control. A remote-controlled toy plane or drone will generally shut itself off and turn on a beacon when its signal is interrupted—when it flies past the range of its controller, for instance. The Deacons had similarly made it so that a remote-controlled worker, a belty, will stand still and clap.

This way, whatever the cause of the signal interruption, prisoners wouldn't end up going very far and—applauding all the while—would be easy to locate.

Ivan had ended up a belty because he'd made the mistake of trying to organize his co-workers to protest the punishment of some low-rank employees in his department who'd been blamed for a satellite systems failure. The workers had been found guilty without a fair trial and had been sentenced to collar-camp internment.

It seemed a shockingly harsh punishment, especially considering that they appeared to be entirely innocent. From what he could tell, the entire situation had been the fault of a higher-up administrator.

Ivan had been very careful. He'd done all his online research at a public terminal, and met with sympathetic colleagues only in person and in private collocation areas. But he had been foolish not to realize the extent to which *everything* he did was being monitored.

POP (the Public Operations Panel) had secret cameras, microphones, and identification trackers *everyplace.* And so, the moment he began to write up a communication that would have embarrassed his supervisors into taking action, he was promptly—without even being given a chance to say goodbye to his family—packed off to a collar camp himself.

After almost two years of hard labor, he had been approached by a Commonplace agent and—despite the obvious perils—agreed to escape.

"In the end," he said of his defection, "it really wasn't . . . a choice. . . . Better a . . . paraplegic . . . fighter than a . . . remote-controlled . . . zombie doing . . . the bidding of . . . a bunch of . . . techno-Nazis."

My-Chale and a team of commandos had engineered a series of explosions at the Northifornian military base Ivan's crew had been dismantling. In the confusion that followed, they carried Ivan off, leaving the wardens with the impression that Ivan had been entirely obliterated by one of the blasts.

They'd gone to such lengths to recruit Ivan because his skills and knowledge were incredibly valuable. He'd been a very highly placed systems programmer for MIM, the Ministry of Infrastructure and Manufacturing, and knew the workings of many of the Deacons' informational networks. He'd been the principal engineer of the rolling PSN blackouts that knocked out the Deaconry's satellites and drones. This was how, from time to time, the Commonplacers were able to move about without being detected. And it was he who had taught the Commonplacers how to jail-break binkies and prevent them from being tracked.

The Deacons kept patching the holes he'd created, but so far he was still managing to find new ways to disrupt their systems. The only thing he hadn't made any significant progress toward was finding a way to free himself from his collar.

And so the man had been clapping for the entire two years since the Commonplacers had taken him from the work camp. The sad fact was that without an expert in nanotechnology and a lot of high-end surgical equipment, nobody was going to be able to remove a MoK collar without killing its owner. The cruel devices had been designed by the Deacons' scientists to that very end.

His collar's signal blocked by a simple sheet of lead foil, Ivan had become somewhat accustomed to living like this. He was completely paralyzed below the neck other than for clapping. And speaking was difficult. Though he could form words, the problem was that he couldn't make his diaphragm draw breaths to propel more than a few words at a time.

He was strapped to a nearly vertical motorized gurney that he steered around using a voice-control app he'd programmed into his specially configured binky. And otherwise, he told Oma and Patrick, his companion took care of everything.

"Seth!" he barked.

"Yes, master," came the familiar sarcastic voice from a speaker on the side of Ivan's motor-gurney.

"Guests here! . . . Come!"

"Yes, master," said the sarcastic voice.

"Seth's a . . . joker," said Ivan. "Thinks that . . . 'master' crap . . . is funny."

"Not as funny as speaking three words every ten minutes,"

said a voice behind them. Oma and Patrick turned to see a big gorilla wearing Wayfarer sunglasses and with enormous bat wings tucked against his back.

He was, Patrick decided, somehow both more and less alarming than the flying monkeys in *The Wizard of Oz*.

"You guys want some soda?" Seth asked.

"Sure," said Patrick. He was pretty thirsty and also tired of drinking water from ponds, puddles, and streams. The Deacons had destroyed all harmful bacteria and parasites, so nothing was unsafe with the practice. But it didn't make it taste any better.

"What's soda?" asked Oma.

"Bubbly water, often infused with a syrup of some kind—for flavor," explained Seth.

"We have a great collection of old syrup and CO_2 canisters and can make marvelous grape, orange, cola, and Dr Pepper–flavored beverages if you like," said Seth.

"Oooh—I'll take Dr Pepper," said Patrick. "Please."

Oma seemed mystified.

"Get orange," said Patrick. "Everybody likes orange."

"Hey, that's true. I don't know anybody who doesn't like orange soda," Seth said over his shoulder as he knuckle-walked out of the room.

"He's actually . . . wonderful," said Ivan, looking past his clapping hands at the empty doorway where Seth had just disappeared. "Whatever happens . . . don't ever . . . get a collar . . . waking nightmare. . . . Bright side is . . . I can drink . . . soda and never . . . get fat . . . due to the clapping. . . . It's good exercise."

"It sounds awful," said Oma. Patrick knew she was terrified of—and fascinated by—MoK collars. "Does it hurt?"

"Hurts like a thousand . . . ice cream headaches . . . when they first . . . put it on. . . . It's the long-term . . . that gets you. . . . Imagine everything . . . your body does . . . being done by . . . somebody else."

"Sounds like torture to me," said Patrick.

"Pure and simple," agreed Ivan. "Makes for a . . . cheap labor source . . . though."

"How do you stay sane?" asked Oma.

"I work!" shouted the man. "I work all day . . . all night. . . . I work without . . . being able to . . . draw my own breath . . . or move my limbs. . . . I work my mind. . . . I work my mouth. . . . I work poor Seth. . . . I work machines. . . . I work asleep. . . . Can't tell you how many . . . ideas come while dozing. . . . If you believe . . . in your work . . . it gets done."

"Honestly," he continued with a nod at Oma, "if not for the . . . Commonplace, my . . . mind . . . would be . . . lost."

"Let's have our soda pop!" said Seth, bounding back into the room with three plastic tumblers of liquid.

Oma sipped cautiously. "This is *good!*" Her next sip was far less cautious.

Patrick figured it was no surprise that a girl who'd been raised on health food would enjoy soda.

"Orange soda. There's no other beverage like it," pronounced Seth.

"You're tired?" said Ivan. "Want to sleep . . . or talk plans? . . . We've hatched a . . . worthy one."

Oma and Patrick looked at each other and nodded. They'd

both managed to sleep on My-Chale's back last night. Also, because they were both holding just-started sodas, they figured they might as well hear what the clapping man had to say. He did seem rather excited.

"Great," he said, eyes twinkling. "Seth, bring prison . . . suits and . . . MoK collars, please!"

CHAPTER 26

Another Journey by Train

OLD ICHABOD COFFIN GOT ON THE TRAIN TO NEW York City, where he meant to get a new iPhone and a good lunch. Generally the train wasn't very crowded in the late morning like this, but today was St. Patrick's Day, and although there was only one more stop before the Hedgerow Heights station, it was already nearly filled with people dressed in green heading into the city to see the parade. Still, he was able to find a seat in his favorite car—the last one, the quiet car.

Ichabod stuck his round-trip ticket in the slot on the seat ahead of him and, since his iPhone was out of commission, unfolded the *New York Times* he'd purchased at the concession stand. He reflected that he hadn't read an actual newspaper in years and that he hadn't missed the dry, powdery feel of the gray paper one bit.

He was reading a story on closing libraries when the young man behind him began a rather loud conversation on his cell phone, which he had in speaker mode.

"Yo, Terry! Whassup!??" said the voice on the phone.

Ichabod turned his hearing aids down all the way but it was no help.

"YEAH, R-TRAP," replied the young man, rather loudly. "I JUST GOT ON THE TRAIN. YOU GET OFF WORK OKAY? ARE THE LOVELY HANNAH AND HER FRIENDS MEETING US AT MULDOON'S?!"

"Do you mind!?" said Ichabod, standing and turning around, but the young man refused to make eye contact.

Being ignored like this infuriated Ichabod. He folded his newspaper and began waving it, driving a not-quite-stiff breeze across the young man's face as he replied to a series of hooting noises from his phone. Whomever he was speaking to appeared to think that "BWAAAP!" was a word.

"YEAH, IT'S GOING TO BE B-I-G HUGE!" the young man said in reply.

"This is the *quiet car*," said Ichabod, not accepting defeat. Two years ago, to offset the growing incivility of people just like this young man, the train authority had designated the northernmost car of each train a quiet car—phone calls were prohibited and conversation even between two people was to be kept to a minimum.

"YO, POPS, POP A SQUAT!" said the young man. Other people, many also wearing green, began to stare.

A burst of indignant-sounding *BWAAP*s and *WOOOK*s came out of the phone.

"JUST SOME OLD DUDE GETTIN' IN MY FACE," said the young man, turning his Boston Celtics baseball cap backward and scrunching down in his seat. "YEAH, YEAH," he continued. "HE'S ALL FLUSTICATED NOW, TURNING PURPLE AND SH—"

Ichabod grabbed his ticket and stormed out of his seat and down the aisle. He had earlier spotted the conductor at the very end of the car in her little booth.

Responding to Ichabod's sharp-knuckled knockings, a harried-looking conductor in what looked to be her late fifties swung open the door and gave him a weary blink.

"Can I help you," she said more than asked as she replaced the mesh cap on her head.

"There's a young man in this car talking on his cell phone very loudly and he *won't* stop!" said Ichabod.

"Oh," said the conductor. "So?"

"Well, can you come ask him to stop? I confronted him about his behavior and he was downright rude in return. I mean, what's the point of having a quiet car if nobody pays attention to the—"

"It's not a quiet car," interrupted the conductor.

"What do you mean?" asked Mr. Coffin. "It's the northern-most car, the end of the train!"

"Quiet car rules are only in effect during peak hours," said the conductor.

"What?!" said Mr. Coffin, his mind considering whether she might have an interest in lying to him. "Why would they only have it during peak hours?"

"It's for when the trains are crowded, not during the day with irregular riders."

"But that's crazy," said Mr. Coffin. "People are just as rude and loud at noon as they are at nine a.m. or five p.m."

The conductor shrugged and smiled as if to a child who'd just said if everybody would only be nice to each other, there wouldn't be wars.

"I agree—but the rules are the rules," she said. "Look, just go forward another car and find a quieter place to sit. And count yourself lucky it's the morning. You should see the trains coming back this afternoon after the parade. You think this is loud? You won't be able to swing a cat in here without hitting a drunk."

"I'm not *on* an afternoon train and I am going to write an e-mail to the railroad about this situation. Why would you not have a quiet car at all times? Does my fare matter less at ten a.m. than it does at eight a.m.?"

"Actually," said the conductor, smiling, "it does. Peak-hour fares are two dollars more."

Ichabod felt the condescension in her voice. Seething, he jabbed a big-knuckled finger at the name tag on her blue jacket.

"Well, thank you, *Janet K.*," he said. "And thank you for all the information about peak fares, and *cat-swinging*."

"You're funny," she said drily, and closed her door.

He turned and stormed back down the aisle, firmly ignoring

the young man who, still on his phone, broke off from his conversation and said, "Hey, Pops, I saved your seat!"

Ichabod crossed into the next car and, because it contained a bathroom and he could smell it, continued on to the next one, hurrying now because the train was about to stop in Tarrytown and a new flood of paradegoers would be boarding.

He took the first unoccupied window seat on the river side and was just unfolding his *New York Times* when the group in the forward-and-backward-facing seats in front of him—two small children, two middle-sized ones, one teen, a woman, a man, and an old lady—suddenly struck him as familiar. It was his next-door neighbors, the—what was their last name?—Gibbons? Gifford? *Griffin!* That was it! The ones whose son had just gone missing and that the police had asked him about rather than following up on leads about his own recent criminal situation—the forced invasion and near-burgling of his home!

He supposed he felt a little bad over the missing boy. Their tragedy was all over Facebook. But he had always disapproved of them. Between the father with his horribly loud leaf blower and their eldest son always banging away with that obnoxious basketball on their driveway and the older daughter who dressed up like a Satan-worshipping vampire, they were simply a low-class, overbreeding annoyance.

Still, it was interesting to see them up so close. He peered over the top of his paper at the mother, the father, and the grandmother, the one with the ridiculous old French car she was forever driving into his hedge. They were bent toward one another, talking softly and urgently.

He really thought very little of them, but he couldn't help being curious as to what they might be saying. Perhaps it was something about their missing boy? He turned up his hearing aids and leaned forward as he pretended to read his paper.

The first word he heard was "BunBun."

CHAPTER 27

Tryouts for the Human Race

KEMPTON, ON HIS WAY TO SILICON CITY VIA THE windowless UTS (ultrasonic transcontinental shuttle), tried to make conversation with a bored-looking man, his only companion on the flight.

"A kid from my echelon at school got niched by MuK," he said. On not receiving a reply he continued, "His name is Bing Steenslay. Have you ever heard of him? He was called up just last week. He wasn't among my *best* friends, but he was a pretty good guy, I guess. You know, he might be curious to learn I had the Earthling, Patrick Griffin, borrow a change of clothes from his locker. Of course he wouldn't mind because of course when you get niched you get your own new uniform and things—like yours, I mean. Is that what everybody in the Ministry of Communications wears—all gray and white like that? It's pretty nice-looking, really."

The young steward sighed and clamped his binky over his eyes.

Kempton sighed, too. They were two deuces into the hypersonic flight to Silicon City. Things were starting to feel a little weightless, which meant the ramjet-powered aircraft was reaching its apogee, crossing into the lower regions of outer space before the rapid descent to Southifornia.

Kempton shrugged and put his own binky over his face. The VR-mode games weren't as robust as they were with a proper holographic gaming room, but it was better than nothing. He decided to play something a little low-effects, like WCL 50, the latest World Champions' League game.

He was just refining his player's attributes—he preferred intimidating mass and upper-body strength over agility or speed—when an incoming message alert flared at the edge of his screen. He expanded the comm app and saw the message alert, once again a priority level 1 from MuK, the Ministry of Communications. His whole body tingled with excitement as he read the message:

sitizen <u>pü</u>ber, fə<u>miL</u>ɛərɪz yor<u>seL</u>f wið ðis skript. re<u>kord</u>ing <u>se</u>ʃən tü bɛ<u>gin</u> im<u>mɛd</u>ɛətɪy ə<u>pon</u> yur ar<u>rɪv</u>əL.

But his enthusiasm collapsed into confusion as he read the attached document. What they were asking him to say didn't make any sense.

CHAPTER 28

Back to Camp

PATRICK AND OMA FINISHED THEIR SODAS AS THEY regarded the prisoner uniforms and MoK collars Seth placed on the table in front of them.

"My-Chale hatched . . . plan when . . . you arrived," Ivan said to Patrick.

"It's not at all unlike BunBun's mission on Earth when you think about it," said Seth.

"It's all about . . . awareness," added Ivan.

"To take a *Commonplace* entry a step further," said Seth, "we must not only rouse ourselves from the half-slumber the average person lives in, but we must rouse the average person, too."

"Stiv Bators . . . said it best," said Ivan, and then sang, confined to the beat of his clapping, a few halting lines from some song that involved opening eyes and lies.

"He was a Lord of the New Church, that Stiv," said Seth.

Neither Oma nor Patrick had any idea what they were talking about.

"So, wait," said Oma, "what part do we play in this?"

"We need . . . Patrick to . . . speak straight . . . to the people," said Ivan.

"What do I say?"

"Something that gets them to question the world around them, and the Deacons' role in it," said Seth.

"Yes," said Ivan. "You need . . . to plant doubt. . . . Get them . . . to ask questions . . . they haven't . . . considered."

"Like," said Oma, "if Rex rescued the world from the Stone Age, why are there abandoned cities around the world that the Deacons don't let anybody know about?"

"If I could . . . meaningfully . . . applaud," said Ivan, "I would."

"Or you could perhaps point out the hidden microphones and cameras they have in places they assure us are private," said Seth.

"Or tell them how innocent people are forced to wear MoK collars," said Oma.

"Or how Rex isn't dead and in fact is back here on Ith at this very moment," said Seth.

"It's true, then?" said Patrick. "The dream My-Chale and I had?"

"Yes," said Seth. "Either it was his plan all along, or perhaps

142

your own transubstantiation to and from Earth prompted him to come back. Either way, he's hiding out in Silicon City, and only his highest administrators—the Deacons, the Seer herself, a select few others—seem to know he's back. We suspect he's waiting for the fiftieth anniversary of his first arrival to do a public announcement."

"Three days from now, Primuary first," said Oma.

"Presumably," said Seth, "he'll also then explain how he's managed to come back from the dead. Wow the populace with some truly Biblical story. They'll probably say the Minder himself brought him back from the dead. It'll be the biggest thing since the Second Coming. The public relations moment of all public relations moments. He'll boost his rep from legend to full-on deity status."

"Unless somebody blows the moment for him," said Oma.

"Precisely right, young woman," said Seth.

"So how do we do it? asked Patrick. "You want me to just record a statement and upload it? 'Hey, everybody—the Deacons and Rex are evil bionic freaks who lie and break the Twelve Tenets on a daily basis!' "

"Yes," said Seth, "as you rightly suspect, it's a bit more complicated than that."

"But not . . . hopelessly so," said Ivan.

"The Deacons," said Seth, "have built safeguards to keep somebody from just posting the truth with a couple clicks. Ivan's been able to hack a lot of systems, but there are crazy redundancies around any wide-scale live feeds. Seriously, to do a broadcast that reaches the full population, you need *manual* activation at no fewer than three priority stations. And it has to be accompanied by a live, in-studio emergency announcement."

"What?" said Patrick. He was pretty sure he'd understood less than one tenth of all that.

"Houses of lies are more delicate than those built on truth," said Seth. "And they know it. They have taken steps to ensure the system can't easily be brought down on their heads.

"They want only their command structure to have access to the proverbial microphone. Only officials in emergency broadcast centers can initiate a wide-scale transmission."

"But," said Oma, "you're saying there's still a way?"

"Yes," said Ivan. "We've figured . . . a work-around. The tough part . . . is getting you . . . to a broadcast center."

"I'm guessing it's probably a little less crazy than traveling back and forth between two worlds?" asked Patrick.

"A degree, perhaps," said Seth. "At least it involves a science we can explain, versus one that we can't."

"Try us," said Oma.

CHAPTER 29
Cherchez Le Bunnyman

TWO DOLLARS AND SEVENTY-FIVE CENTS!" ICHABOD
Coffin exclaimed to the ticket clerk in his tightly sealed booth. "It's a subway, not a hansom cab!"

The man gave him a look a degree more glassy than the bulletproof partition between them.

Coffin swallowed his indignation and passed the man a ten-dollar bill to cover the round-trip fare.

"What do I do with this?" he asked, looking at the card he received along with his change. The last time he'd ridden a New York City subway it had taken tokens.

"PUUTH WINN BRRRHNSTIIIIE," came the man's amplified voice.

"What?!" said Coffin, nervously looking around.

"SWYEPPPP BRRBB DA SSSSSSSSS," said the clerk's voice, pantomiming something with his hand. It looked to Coffin like the man was pretending to feed a goat, but he didn't bother asking again. He could see the family coming now, emerging from the ceramic-tile-lined passageway from the train terminal, all eight of them. Unlike almost everybody else in the terminal, none of them, he noticed now, was wearing St. Patrick's Day green.

He hurried away from the clerk's window, only briefly minding the woman in line behind him grumbling, "It's about time."

He didn't want to talk to his neighbors; he just wanted to follow them. Which shouldn't be too hard since he knew where they were going.

As he'd heard the mother explain three times on the train, they were first going to the American Museum of Natural History, then—after the hotel's three p.m. check-in time and provided they hadn't found any leads—to their reserved rooms at the Seventh Avenue Hilton, where they would deposit the twins and the grandmother.

From there he'd have to decide which group to follow because the rest of them were going to break up into two teams: the mother and the weird oldest daughter on one, and the father and the two younger daughters on the other.

The mother's thinking—with which Mr. Coffin could find no fault—went that this BunBun rabbit-man had obviously been headed south.

Though he hadn't overheard the full conversation, Mr. Coffin gleaned that the villainous rabbit-man was heading to Midtown Manhattan.

It seemed rather bizarre, but then the entire week had strained belief as far as Mr. Coffin was concerned. And here, at least, was a thread of sense: the family that lived next door to him had lost their son at the very moment when his house had been burgled by this very same BunBun.

The police had not come close to solving either crime despite all the evidence and cooperation he and the neighbor family had given them. Honestly, how were they, himself included, *not* to take matters into their own hands at this point?

The adults were using their fare cards—swiping them through the turnstile slots—to let the children through. Mr. Coffin understood now what it was the ticket clerk had been pantomiming and also that he had better get moving if he was going to get aboard the same shuttle train. A line six green-wearing people deep had already formed behind the family.

Palming his fare card, Mr. Coffin emerged from his hiding place around the side of the ticket booth and, as he got in line, one of the little twins spotted him.

"Old neighbor man!" yelled young Cassie Griffin, pointing right at him.

CHAPTER 30
Bridge & Tunnel

BUNBUN PLUNGED INTO THE MURKY DEPTHS OF the Harlem River and swam for all he was worth, which—despite his general exhaustion—was quite a lot. His big feet and impressive lung capacity meant he could have swum the length of five Olympic swimming pools entirely underwater, and twice as fast as even the great Michael Phelps.

Unseen by the police and the bewildered witnesses on the Broadway Bridge, he made landfall on the island of Manhattan just above the 207th Street subway yard. He quickly clambered up the steep, debris-strewn bank and leapt the barbed-wire fence, dodged between stationary subway cars, and disappeared into an unlit rail tunnel with a spray-painted sign that read, "A Train access, call dispatch before proceeding."

"What luck," he said to himself as he bounded into the darkness. "If I recall my map studies correctly, the A Train should get me nearly there!"

CHAPTER 31
Flight Connection

NEIL HAD A DISCONCERTING DREAM, ESPECIALLY considering it involved being on an airplane while he was in fact *on* an airplane.

In it, he was sitting across the aisle from a hooded charac-ter. The flight attendant with the drink cart came up the aisle and stopped in front of the hooded figure across from Neil.

"Sir," said the beverage server, "can I get you something to drink?"

"I wish," replied the hooded figure, his voice somehow sounding like swarming bees, "to have the blood of a freshly killed lamb, stirred with the jawbone of an, erm"—and here the hooded figure turned to look at Neil, revealing only darkness beneath the folds of his gray cowl—"donkey."

Neil woke with a start and looked around. There was an old woman in the aisle seat where the hooded figure had been. He took a moment to calm himself down, to reassure himself that *obviously* it had just been a dream—nothing at all bad was really going on around him. Or, at least, nothing so weird as that.

He was still sitting next to Uncle Andrew and the talkative man in the window seat, the man with the gold chain and the bushy gray hair and the enormous fingers with the similarly enormous gold rings upon them.

"The problem with classical," the man was just saying, "is that it's all cover music."

Uncle Andrew, in the middle seat, nodded and laughed. The two of them were on their second whiskey on the rocks. Uncle Andrew had excused himself to Neil on that score, explaining that flying made him nervous. This had prompted the big-fingered man—Dave Murphy, a librarian from Poughkeepsie—to say he felt the same way. And so now Neil was stuck right next to two bonding, whiskey-drinking, and increasingly loud dudes who hated to fly.

Flying didn't make Neil nervous. He'd only been on two plane trips before, but he enjoyed the experience. Or, at least, he had until this flight.

Beyond having them to listen to, he now had nothing to do but read the super-lame airline magazine. And somebody had done all the puzzles in it already. He scrunched down even farther in his seat to stew about the life decisions he'd made to get him to this point where he had no smartphone and no way of playing a game or even watching YouTube.

"Think about it. To be originals, you'd need Beethoven or what's-his-name, Mozart up there on stage or in the studio. That crap—pardon my French, young man," the man named Dave said, looking over at Neil, "is all a big scam, orchestrated—pardon the pun—by the Violin Manufacturing Consortium."

Uncle Andrew found this to be very funny.

"So, what are you guys doing in Texas, Andrew?" said Dave the librarian, realizing he'd not asked one of the more fundamental questions of air-travel companionship.

Uncle Andrew opened his mouth and closed it, taking another sip from his drink before replying, "Well, Dave, we're going to Corpus Christi to try to see that French woman," he said.

"The Miracle Woman?!" said Dave.

Uncle Andrew and Neil both nodded.

"Ain't that the darnedest story you ever heard? I love her pluck, refusing to leave the church, even as all the media elites line up to say it's a hoax.

"What," he continued, "kind of crazy hoax takes an old lady from France and puts her in southern Texas? I mean, it doesn't even make any sense. If it were a scam, they would have put her in some holy site in the Middle East or something. I mean, a Roman Catholic miracle that involves *Texas*?

"Plus," he continued, "seems just a bit past crazy how people keep implying she's some kind of degenerate. I mean, an eighty-year-old retired foreign language teacher from rural France is suddenly some sort of scam artist? And she's asking that people make donations to the church? Where's the big dark agenda there? Follow the non-money, people!"

"Does seem to raise some questions," said Uncle Andrew.

"Never mind the conspiracy theories—do you boys think it's actually a holy miracle of some kind? Is that why you're headed down?"

"Not exactly," said Uncle Andrew, thoughtful all of a sudden.

"Sorry, didn't mean to pry," said the man.

"No, that's okay," said Uncle Andrew. "We have a family member who had something similar happen to him. Disappeared from his home in a flash and apparently ended up on another continent."

"Get out!" said the man, causing the woman sitting ahead of him to peer over her seat back. "Ooops, sorry—*that* was a little loud. Sorry, folks, Jim Beam's messing with my volume knob. But, you're serious?"

"Unfortunately, yes," said Uncle Andrew. "He disappeared from his home just like she did and then—two days later, the same day this woman disappeared from France—he called home, saying he was in France."

Neil shot Uncle Andrew a questioning look: Should he be telling all this to a stranger? Hadn't Mom and everybody agreed that the plan was not to tell *anybody*?

Uncle Andrew gave his nephew a reassuring wink from behind his nerdy rectangular glasses.

"You said it was a family member?" asked Dave.

"Yes, my nephew, brother to Neil here."

"Aw, *man*," said the man, reaching over and patting Neil's knee. "Your brother? That's tough. I'm sorry, little dude."

153

Neil nodded, disconcerted at the sensation of welling tears.

"And the cops don't have any leads?" continued the man.

"Not a one," said Uncle Andrew. "They can't seem to find the phone record of his call to his parents. Even though both parents spoke to him and everybody in the house heard the phone ring."

"That's just about the weirdest thing I've ever heard," said Dave, chewing on his lip.

"Well, anyhow, that's why we're going down. We just want to speak to the French woman, see if she knows anything about Neil's brother Patrick."

"That could be tough getting through to her, though, right?" asked Dave. "I mean, aren't there pilgrims coming in from all over? People sleeping on the sidewalk lining up to have her touch them and all that?"

"Yeah, we figured we'd just get in line like everybody else."

"Well, I was going down to do some fishing with my sister, but I know some folks of importance down there working for the city of Corpus Christi. Let me see if I can't pull some strings for you."

"That'd be very kind of you, Dave," said Uncle Andrew.

"And there's something else. I wasn't always a librarian," Dave said. "I used to work for the federal government, just like you."

"Not DARPA?" asked Uncle Andrew, referring to the research organization where he was employed as a chemist.

"No," replied Dave. "FBI."

CHAPTER 32
Signal Found

VAN, OMA, PATRICK, AND SETH SPENT THE DAY AT the school, napping fitfully, and then, when the sun went down, they set off on foot toward the emergency broadcast center. The complex was located on a reclaimed piece of land in the shadow of Mount Rainier, down close to where the city of Tacoma had once been.

Shortly before dawn, Ivan, strapped to Seth's broad, hairy back, announced that they were close. "Put me down . . . and take . . . off the foil . . . please."

"Oh . . . wow," he exclaimed as Seth unwrapped the signal-blocking foil from his collar. His clapping arms immediately fell to his sides and his legs began kicking. "Oh . . . *ow!*" he said softly. "Oh boy . . . I have not . . . used . . . these muscles . . . in a long . . . time. Ow! . . . Ow! . . . Ow!" he said, clearly in a lot of pain—his face bright red and his eyes wincing—but not screaming somehow.

"Now," he persevered, "let's . . . just hope . . . the patches . . . I made in . . . the system . . . keep my . . . sudden . . . return . . . to the . . . control grid . . . from being . . . noticed.

"You better," he continued, "put me down . . . and get out . . . of sight . . . Seth. . . . The sun's . . . almost up. . . . You saw that . . . storm sewer . . . back there? . . . My pack . . . too, please."

"Yeah, all right," said Seth, putting a small canvas pack on Ivan's back and giving his friend's remotely controlled body a hug. Then he gently patted Oma and Patrick on their heads. "Take care, okay?"

Oma and Patrick nodded.

"Hey!" Seth said to them. "That was a test—you can't nod anymore, right?!"

As Ivan had explained, nods and head shakes relied upon muscles and nerves that extend below the collar, so belties are unable to do either unless specifically instructed by the controlling algorithm. Which they probably never would be since nobody cares to know a belty's opinion on anything anyhow.

"Sorry," said Patrick.

"Stay focused and keep a low profile," continued Seth.

In the meantime, Ivan—or, at least, his body—had begun

to walk west. "Just do . . . exactly as I . . . do," said Ivan through gritted teeth. "If I start . . . going faster . . . you start . . . going faster. . . . If I turn . . . left . . . you turn . . . left . . . et cetera."

"Okay," said Oma. "Are you okay, Ivan?"

"Well . . . it just so happens . . . most of . . . my body is . . . being run by a . . . computer program . . . and it basically . . . feels like my . . . leg muscles . . . are being . . . torn to shreds . . . side effect of not . . . having used them . . . but I'll be . . . fine. Let's . . . get this over . . . with and go . . . fix the world . . . shall we? . . . Here, shall we . . . sing 'The . . . Battle Hymn . . . of the . . . Disempowered . . . Public'?"

"No, no, no!" shouted Seth. "No singing. We've got a hard enough time as it is, you broken windbag of a man."

"That's not . . . nice," said Ivan, smiling.

"Now," said Seth. "All of you. Go and kick some butt." He gave Ivan a hug that the man couldn't return. Then the winged monkey turned, flapped his wings, and flew off to the east.

"He's a . . . good fellow," said Ivan. "Now . . . it's true . . . I can't . . . make much . . . music . . . in my . . . condition. . . . Can either . . . of you . . . whistle . . . something to . . . march to?"

"How's this?" said Oma, and launched into a pitch-perfect and impressively loud tune that Patrick recognized from choir practice: "The Battle Hymn of the Republic."

As the sun rose over the mountains behind them and began to warm their shoulders, he couldn't help feeling inspired.

And he leapt in—at least as best he could remember the lyrics—and began to sing his favorite verse:

"I can read a righteous sentence,
by the dim and flaring lamps
our truth is marching on.
Glory, glory, hallelujah!"

CHAPTER 33
Justice Blind

FROM THE ONE-HUNDRED-TWELFTH-FLOOR WINDOW of the MuK tower where he was being interrogated, Kempton looked up at One Deacon Plaza, the tallest building on Ith, and wondered what it would be like to look down from its rooftop observation deck. He imagined he wouldn't actually feel too much more sick to his stomach than he did right now. He'd been so excited about his trip to Silicon City to have a personal interview with Sabrina Kim, one of Ith's twelve Deacons. He and his parents had figured that his unique experience with the Earthling, Patrick Griffin, was the reason behind it. It was Kempton's opportunity to help with the investigation into Patrick's, and his sister's, disappearance.

But the script he had received on the flight had turned all his excitement into confusion and dread.

And a two-hour session with a Grade-1 emo counselor had done almost nothing to make him feel any better. The simple situation was that he was alone without a person he knew and was about to do something that positively made him want to throw up.

It wasn't that he didn't understand the reason they wanted him to do it. They believed his sister had been brainwashed. And that she had then helped convince Patrick Griffin to join *the Anarchists.*

In other words, they'd both been turned. And this made sense to Kempton. His sister had been acting more and more strangely in recent months. And it also explained why Patrick hadn't seemed more freaked out (like Kempton himself had been) when an enormous Class II Abomination had torn off the roof of the house to kidnap him in the middle of the night.

He could accept all that, even though it did make him and his family seem a little stupid for not realizing they were harboring two criminals. But, again, it wasn't the *why* of the Deacons' plan that freaked him out. It was the *what.*

They wanted him to go on the Seer's Feed, the main world-wide broadcast, received by every Interverse-linked device on the planet, and admit that he—Kempton Puber—*had been a part of the conspiracy to brainwash Patrick Griffin!*

Of course, it was just acting. And he was assured that once his sister and Patrick were returned, his role would be made clear and he'd be awarded a medal for civic duty.

But, until that happened, he would be a pariah to every person he'd ever known.

He couldn't even tell his parents what was going on. The presentation, the agents explained, had to be 100 percent convincing and consistent.

There was no getting out of it. Deacon Sabrina Kim herself had issued the directive, and so not just Tenet Six, "Respect Directives," but Tenet Twelve, "Disobey the Minder's Emissaries in Nothing," was at stake. Breaking a single tenet was grounds for being sent to a collar camp. The penalty for breaking two was rumored to be serving as bait in an Abomination Redress mission. Basically, getting chained out in the wilderness to entice a human-eating monster into the open where it could get captured. Hopefully before it had a chance to eat him.

But by doing what they were telling him to do, he was going to have to be sent to a collar camp anyhow. After his confession, everybody would believe he was a lying traitor and an agent of the worst evil the Three Worlds had ever known. *And they'd all expect him to be severely punished for it.*

That was the key, the SiOps agent had explained last night. Kempton's incarceration—and the terrifying punishment he was to receive—was the psychological lever by which the Deacons could begin to bend back the loyalties, sympathies, and motivations of his sister, Patrick Griffin, and all their PR-conscious handlers.

"That's the Anarchists' whole play," the agent had said. "They seek to undermine all the good that Rex, the Seer, and the Minder have done by subverting the good hearts and minds of our honest, fair-minded fellow citizens. They speak of freedom and wisdom as if it were something we don't possess ourselves, as if the Deacons were controllers rather than stewards, and they themselves defenders of liberty.

"But the thing is," the woman had gone on, "while we can objectively see it's just a scheme, it's a reasonably clever one and can fool many low-scoring citizens. Your sister, not being the highest-performing child—as is obvious from her academic record—was, for instance, easily ensnared by their propaganda.

"And Patrick Griffin," the agent had continued, "being at an educational deficit—coming from a world free from the Anarchist menace—was additionally susceptible."

So the plan was that when Oma and Patrick saw that *he* was being punished for *their* crime, they would feel bad. And this would provide some emotional-motivational leverage for the SiOps agents to win them back over.

He looked at himself in his binky's mirror app. He didn't look bad. Nearly half a dunt with a Ministry of Communications makeup specialist had left him looking almost like one of the dystopian drama—dysma—stars his mother so loved.

But it was faint consolation.

And so this is what he was thinking about as he sat in the spotless, high-tech waiting room outside Sabrina Kim's office, high atop one of the tallest buildings on Ith.

Here he was at the amazing center of everything in the world—Silicon City, the jewel in the crown of humanity's greatest civilization ever—about to destroy his reputation, maybe forever.

He couldn't imagine a more horrible situation. At least until the doors of the executive chamber opened and he beheld the sickening, eyeless face of a Deacon for the first time.

CHAPTER 34
Nine if by Water

WE'RE NUMBATS, NOT OTTERS," SAID SHIFTY, shaking herself dry like a dog. She ended up not so much dry as just less sopping wet.

The numbats had spent the night running along the shore of the Anacostia River. And, where fences, outflows, spotlights, and the occasional security camera necessitated it, they had swum in the river itself.

Numbats are not aquatic but, like most animals, they are capable swimmers when they have to be.

"I think I swallowed some," said Levanty, and sneezed. "It was salty and gross."

"Yuck!" said the ever-tidy Sven.

"You poor thing!" said Shorty. "It smells like pee!"

"It's just tidal," said Barb, "but I agree—I don't want to swim another meter. And, if we were going to cross, we should have done so earlier. In case you haven't noticed, it's gotten pretty wide."

The river had been only as wide as a country road when they'd camped along its bank north of the city limits yesterday. It was now close to half a kilometer across. "I vote we sneak across one of these bridges."

Trixy had been monitoring the binky on Shorty's back and determined that their best chance of getting serious media attention would occur on the other side of the river. That was where most of the pictures and videos were being uploaded to the Internet. That was where the Capitol and the media hot spot called the White House were located, and that was where the organizations that seemed to broadcast the most content were located. ABC, Al Jazeera, CBS, CNN, C-SPAN, Fox News, NBC, NPR, and the *Washington Post* appeared to be what were called "news organizations," and they all seemed to have studios and transmission centers there—places where they recorded and broadcast information to be seen and heard by the rest of the world.

"I vote we swim," said Sven, rotating his arms. "Come on, it's not that far."

"Let's take a bridge," said Barb.

"We can't take a bridge. We'll be spotted by one of those traffic cams," replied Trixy.

"So?" said Barb.

"So, nine numbats running in concerted fashion across a

bridge in an area of the world where they are not indigenous could invite interest. And, remember, until we really want it, we *don't* want to attract attention."

"I'm hungry," said Dirty.

"No, you're Dirty," said Graty, and laughed, looking for somebody to give her a high five. "You see what I did there!? You see, his name's Dirty but he said he was Hungry so I was all, like, 'No you're not!'"

Nobody gave her a high five. The most she got was a groan from Barb.

"There are doughnut shops over there," said Trixy, looking at the map on the binky.

"What's a doughnut shop?" asked Tenty.

"Aren't doughnuts, like, pastries?" asked Shifty, who'd read of them in books.

"Yes," said Trixy, who'd just clicked over to an Internet entry about them. "'Fried, sweetened pieces of generally leavened dough, often made in an O shape and coated with sugar.'"

"Hey, that sounds okay," said Shorty.

"Yes, let's investigate," said Levanty.

"All right," said Sven. "Let's get swimming. We will look for doughnuts on the other side."

"I'm not a child," said Barb. "You guys can't convince me to do things by promising treats. I'm not going in that so-called river again. I am a dry-land animal."

"A dry-land animal!" exclaimed Shifty, and belted out a poem.

"I'm a dry-land animal
I swish my lengthy tail
within the cool clear air
I'm a ground-loving beast
I flap my feet upon the ground
And dive into my lair
But I don't fall when I sit still
So call me plodding if you will—
I'm grounded and don't care!"

Even though she'd been doing this sort of thing all their lives, everybody stared at her like she'd lost her mind.

"*Book of Commonplace*, section 887, paragraph ninety-three," she said triumphantly.

"I know most people don't read enough," said Barb to Shifty. "But *you* read too much."

"Come on," said Sven, marching down the muddy bank to the river, "let's go. There's not much time till the sun's up."

With varying degrees of nonenthusiasm, the other eight followed him into the water.

CHAPTER 35
Convicts & Calendrics

PATRICK, OMA, AND IVAN FOUND THE WORK DETAIL marching across a leveled field of rubble that had once been a town. There were over a hundred belties filing down the roadway, carrying tools ranging from shovels and brooms to jackhammers, leaf blowers, and a few strange high-tech implements that Patrick didn't recognize.

"Good," said Ivan as they caught up with the back of the group. "A big . . . work gang. Our . . . addition won't . . . be so . . . conspicuous. . . . Now, not . . . that it should . . . matter unless guards . . . are around, but . . . you guys . . . should probably . . . make efforts to speak . . . like me. So . . . in case any . . . of the prisoners . . . are aspiring . . . stool pigeons. . . . Best to . . . keep a low . . . profile."

"Patrick," Oma said, "pull down your work cap to cover your ears, and put those safety goggles on so you don't stick out like an alien thumb."

Patrick nodded.

"Hail there . . . stragglers," said a long-bearded, long-haired man as they got close. Actually, all the men had long beards. And everybody had long hair.

"Hail, fellow . . . traitors to the State!" replied Ivan.

"We're all . . . innocent!" said a woman and then also *said*, rather than *laughed*, "Heh, heh . . . heh-heh."

It occurred to Patrick that one couldn't belly-laugh very well. The collars controlled all of a person's muscles from the neck down.

"It's all a big," continued the woman, "clerical mistake. . . . It wasn't me . . . that called . . . my supervisor . . . a donkey pit! . . . I'd never . . . ever-ever . . . do such . . . a thing! . . . We had a . . . directive against . . . insulting our . . . moronic . . . admins, and . . . I'd never . . . ever-ever- . . . ever break . . . Tenet Four! . . . heh-hee . . . ha . . . ho!"

"Amen . . . sister," said another belty, and Ivan did, too.

The conversation petered out then and they marched the next mile in silence.

"Can we talk normally?" Patrick whispered to Oma.

"Not . . . breaking it . . . up . . . you mean?"

"Yeah. It must drive them crazy having to talk like that all the time."

"Yeah, I don't think they need to be driven to Crazy. They've been living there a good long time," Oma whispered back. "Poor things. But I think as long as we whisper they can't hear us back here. And they can't turn their heads around to see we're talking. So let's just try to keep it down. Why, what'd you want to say?"

"Well, one is that they stink," Patrick whispered to Oma.

Oma and Patrick had complained more than once of not having washed since leaving the Pubers' home four days ago. But the two of them smelled like roses next to the work crew they'd just joined.

"Reminds me of that mean kids' birthday song," she replied.

"What song is that?" asked Patrick.

Oma looked around to ensure nobody was listening. She sang softly,

"Happy dirt-day to you,
Happy dirt-day to you,
You smell like a belty
And you'll be one of them soon."

"Wait, what day is it?" asked Patrick.

"Let's see," said Oma. "We left home on Sevensday, you went back to Earth on Onesday . . . it's got to be Foursday," said Oma.

Patrick barely remembered not to put his hands to his face in frustration. He had forgotten that Rex had redone the Ith calendar to make things more efficient. The days of the week here on Ith ran from Onesday to Sevensday rather than from Sunday to Saturday. And the months counted off Primuary, Seconduary, Tertuary, all the way to Dodecuary, which was what it happened to be now. Rex had also had the months and years annualized to the day he first arrived on Ith, and rather than having the years count from AD, the people now counted from the year of his arrival, so it was the year AR (After Rex) forty-nine. And the New Year on Ith happened in what would be March on Earth. In light of all that confusing stuff, he realized he needed to ask the question differently.

"How many days has it been since I got here?" he said.

"Well, Lasters—the day we left—was the twenty-fourth. It's now the twenty-eighth."

"So," said Patrick, thinking out loud, "when I came from Earth, it was Saturday, and I went back on Monday, and then came back, and we've been traveling for three days so . . . it's March seventeenth back home," he said. "St. Patrick's Day."

"What?" asked Oma. "Is that some sort of holiday?"

"Yeah," said Patrick. "And it's actually my birthday."

"Aw," said Oma, not sarcastically at all.

CHAPTER 36
Flushed Out

WHAT A SMALL WORLD," SAID MARY GRIFFIN AS their gawky, peculiar, old-fashioned next-door neighbor emerged from the subway turnstile.

"What brings you to the city, Mr. Coffin?" asked Rick.

The kids stared at the old man with their mouths open as they took in—for the first time up close—the mysterious man from next door. Their eyes lingered on his long, big-knuckled fingers, bulging Adam's apple, liver-spotted forehead, and, especially, the tufts of wiry gray, white, and strangely yellow hairs sprouting from his rather large ears and nose.

Their much more well-preserved grandmother, Nana,

meanwhile took in the quality of his clothes and the entire absence of any rings on his fingers.

Mr. Coffin saw her looking at his hands and found himself self-consciously wondering at the date of his last fingernail trimming. His mother used to always nag him about trimming them and he still—twenty years after her death—would resist the activity till he'd badly snagged a shirt or sweater cuff, or developed a hangnail.

"Yes," repeated Mary, seeing her husband's question was going unanswered, "what brings you to town?"

"I, er, I need to replace my iPhone," he said, "and so I had to come in for that, and to get lunch at the Club."

"What club is that?" asked Nana.

"Er, the Knickerbocker," said Mr. Coffin.

"They have terrific burgers," said Nana, who'd in fact been to the crusty old social club with a man she'd once dated.

"Er, yes, they do," said Mr. Coffin, touching his tie knot as he gave Nana a second look.

"And you take the subway there," said Rick. "I'm impressed."

"Yes, well, er, it's . . . efficient," said Mr. Coffin.

"Well," said Mary, "are you riding the shuttle, too?"

"Yes, isn't the Knickerbocker on Fifth Avenue?" said Nana.

Mr. Coffin blanched. He'd just said he was in the city to go to the Knickerbocker and the Apple Store, and there was of course an Apple Store in Grand Central Terminal where he'd just left, and the shuttle train would take him farther from rather than closer to the Knickerbocker.

He obviously couldn't admit that he had been following them, but since that's just what he wanted to do, he was going to have to think quickly to explain why he was taking this train.

And then, not knowing what came over him, he began to cry. He babbled to them about his stressful week—the burglary, the man in the bunny suit, his drowned phones, his frustrations with the police.

"Yes, we've had a tough week, too," said Mary pointedly, when he finally took a breath.

"Oh, I know," said Mr. Coffin, truly overcome now. "Your—your *son*," he said, and began sobbing so hard that Rick felt compelled to put a steadying hand on the old man's shoulder.

"I wish I could—could help," Mr. Coffin choked out.

"Well, I say the more the merrier," said Nana. "Many hands make light work and all that."

The children and Rick looked at Nana like she was crazy, but Mary rubbed her chin, looked at the red-eyed old man, now blowing his nose into an antique handkerchief, and said, "Well, it just so happens we're here in the city trying to get some questions answered about our missing boy. Since it seems maybe your circumstances are somehow involved with ours, we're happy to have you come along, especially if you think you can pull yourself together and be of some help."

Mr. Coffin hadn't been spoken to like this since his mother was alive and, strangely, it made him feel very happy inside. He nodded and stifled his sobs.

"I would love to help!" he blurted, and looked around at the family gratefully.

"You have hair in your ears," said Cassie, staring up at the old man.

"Like BunBun!" shouted Paul, who thought this was hilarious.

"Cassie and Paul!" scolded Mary Griffin. "We do not talk about other people's physical appearances in public! I'm so sorry, Mr. Coffin. They're just four."

"Not a concern," said Mr. Coffin, straightening up and clearing his throat. "We Coffin men have always had ear wool. Family trait, dates back centuries."

Over to one side, Lucie said, "This day couldn't get any weirder if it tried." Eva and Carly both nodded.

CHAPTER 37
Guaranteed Passage

SETH WAS NOT HAVING A GOOD-LUCK DAY. REX'S order about rounding up all remaining Mindthlings on Ith happened to be put into action that very same day.

In just the past two days they'd commissioned a multi-ministry effort to improve their high-altitude drone and satellite surveillance system, the "sky-eyes," as the common people called them. They'd had anti-hack technicians and troubleshooters increase their hours, reallocated their data servers to run pattern-recognition algorithms, and nearly doubled their drone sweeps in areas where they suspected Anarchist activity.

The long and the short of it was that one of their mid-altitude drones managed to spot the winged gorilla's heat signature just as he approached the drainage culvert where he had been planning to hide for the rest of the day.

A platoon of YSS (Union of Soldiers and Scientists) commandos quickly converged on the location, captured him, and brought him back to a nearby interrogation facility run by INRI—as the enormous flag over the windowless concrete building made clear.

Some very long and nightmarish hours began for Seth then. He was strapped to an X-shaped frame, then portions of him were shaved, and he was systematically prodded, probed, and injected with a wide array of instruments and chemicals.

And then Rex arrived.

Seth at first almost believed that the imposing, short-bearded man in the black turtleneck was just a hallucination. Perhaps it was the drugs they'd given him. Or maybe his brain was short-circuiting due to the pain. But in the end there was no denying the reality of the dark-minded man in front of him.

With all the humor of a second-rate game-show host, Rex said, "You've been a bad monkey, haven't you?"

Seth tried to say something defiant back, but his tongue felt drier than a saltine cracker and all he could think to say was, "Nice turtleneck, you weirdo."

"Look at his spirit, will you?" said Rex, gesturing at Seth as he looked around at the assembled soldiers and interrogation specialists. "Over a dunt's worth of our most effective interrogation techniques, and still he wants to show spirit, wants to show that he's unbroken—that his belief in his cause is so strong and so right that he will fight even as his body is broken.

"Tell me," he said, turning back to Seth, "do you think anybody cares? Do you think anybody is admiring your imagined heroism?"

"I suppose," Seth said slowly, struggling for breath, "it depends on how brainwashed your servants are . . ."

"Yes, go on," said Rex.

"Do . . . ," continued Seth, struggling to speak and thinking of his friend Ivan as he did so. "Do they see me as a creature with feelings and spirit, or am I just . . . a monster?"

He smiled weakly at the yellow-, green-, and blue-suited technicians standing around in their mirrored faceplates.

"Perhaps," said Rex, "these men and women here will be sympathetic—is that what you mean? Or one of the technicians watching the camera feeds? Or do you mean to indicate that somebody or something bigger, somebody more powerful, will admire your strength? Perhaps, even, the consciousness of Mindth will observe your tribulations?"

"If you knew anything about Mindth," said Seth, "you'd be acting very differently."

"*I,*" said Rex, "happen to know more about Mindth than anybody on Ith *or* Earth."

Seth closed his eyes and winced as a new pain clawed its way up his spine.

"Believing in the mythical power of that world like you idiots do," continued Rex, "is exactly the sort of naive, childish vision that has forever doomed humankind to famine, war, poverty, and darkness."

"Because believing in something . . . bigger than yourself . . . is so bad for people?" said Seth, smiling wryly despite the pain in his eyes.

"Yes, believing in the *wrong* bigger thing is in fact quite bad for people," replied Rex, "especially when the belief serves as a form of self-medication."

"So . . . ," said Seth, nodding at the IV tube running into his arm, "as long as you're medicating somebody else . . . it's okay. Right?"

"That? Why, we're just helping you remain as lucid as possible. Don't want you falling asleep on us while we're giving you a chance to undo the harm you've done.

"Now," Rex continued, "are you going to help us find the Earthling, or do we need to raise your dosage?"

The winged ape made his eyes as large as he could and cocked his head like a curious puppy. "Is this Heaven?"

"You are a blessed individual, it's true," said Rex. He turned to the technician in the blue hooded outfit.

The technician nodded and tapped her BNK-E screen.

The IV drip going into Seth's arm sped up.

The lead technician stood back from Seth, and in a moment the winged ape's body convulsed. His bat-like wings snapped free of their restraints, extending fully outward, flapping once, twice, three times.

And then stopped beating and drooped to the floor.

An alarm tone began to sound.

"Turn that off!" barked Rex. "We've concluded our little

experiment here. Tell Karen Grace and William George to activate and deploy all of the ARS reserves. It's time to harvest the Mindthlings. All of them."

Seth's body then lost color and came apart, falling through his restraints like powdered glass.

"There's no question," Rex said as he watched the silvery substance fall to the ground, "we are going to need all the transcense we can get."

Two gray-suited technicians, wearing caps that read **T.R.y.**, rushed forward with a cylindrical device that proceeded to vacuum up what had once been Seth.

CHAPTER 38
Take the A Train

BEFORE VERY LONG, THE SERVICE TUNNEL FROM the subway yard intersected the active, north-south running A-Train line.

Mr. BunBun remembered from the maps he'd studied on his binky two neighborhoods in particular, Times Square and Rockefeller Center. Both appeared to have an especially high concentration of significantly attended media transmissions and appeared to be good places to be to ensure that when he came out in public, he would really come out in public.

Now he just needed to get there, and this subway tunnel seemed to offer—despite the bad smells, pools of disgusting water, and several large trains to avoid—a convenient and stealthy way to do so. If Rex's high-tech minions were monitoring cameras, satellites, and communications feeds scouring the surface of the world for him, then it was a good thing to be below the surface in a tunnel meant only for trains.

As far as the trains went, it was pretty easy to tell when one was coming and get out of the way. The first station he reached, Dyckman Street, had posed a bit of a problem—there were people waiting for trains on elevated platforms on both sides, and he couldn't very well just stroll down the track without them seeing him. But he soon discovered that when one train stopped, there was just enough room to hurry along its side, right next to the wheels and beneath the platform, and in that way he could move past the platforms unseen.

And so, trying not to think about rat poop and filthy pools of garbage-filled, foul-smelling water—which he sometimes had to step in—he made it down past 190th, 181st, 175th, 163rd, 155th, all the way to 81st Street before he made something of a mistake.

Failing to notice the conductor in the back of the platformed train ahead of him, he allowed her to snap his picture through the back door window of her little compartment. The flash of her smartphone so surprised him that he wondered if he'd accidentally stepped on the electrified third rail. He froze like a piece of museum taxidermy until he'd heard his heart beat once, twice, three times. He didn't look around to piece together what had happened, and by then it was too late.

From the conductor's perspective, the flash reflected on the window glass and produced a rather blurry, indistinct image. But, in the picture she transmitted to her supervisor—and then to her mother and sister—his antlers and general shape were clearly discernible.

And not just to the message's intended recipients.

CHAPTER 39

The Rules of Transubstantiation, Refined

WITHIN SECONDS, BUNBUN'S FUZZY, OVEREXPOSED snapshot was brought to the attention of Victor Pierre, acting president of worldwide operations for Kingaroo and Rex's appointed leader of the 119 Deaconry candidates remaining here on Earth.

The harsh-faced man had been monitoring a lab test from behind a double-paned laboratory observation window, but he paused to regard the image and note where it had been taken.

"Yes, that's the enemy combatant," he said, agreeing with the mid-level official who had escalated the picture to his attention.

He issued a single mental command instructing the nearest

two emergency response teams to converge on the A-Train subway tunnels between 86th and 72nd Streets.

As the metadata indicated, the creature appeared to be a Class III, and one without any particularly impressive physical features. Its antlers were hardly big enough to impale a chicken, and otherwise, one assumed, its biggest offensive threat was its large hind legs.

Which wasn't to say the creature should be underestimated. Obviously—having eluded agents over the course of five days now—it was well trained and not stupid. But Victor Pierre wasn't too worried that it would manage to distract him much longer.

He turned his attention back to the laboratory experiment unfolding in front of him. A rhesus monkey wearing a little yellow biohazard suit was secured to a metal trellis along the far wall of the test chamber. In the middle of the room, a cylinder about the size of a big coffee thermos sat at the center of a web of hoses and wires. The lid began to turn, unscrewing itself. A black substance oozed out of the gap and onto the rubberized floor.

The monkey began to scream now—not that it was audible to Victor in the soundproofed observation room, but he could tell. The creature's mouth and panicked eyes were wide against the plastic faceplate of its little yellow suit.

The black substance spreading across the floor almost resembled some sort of oily sludge except that it had a dull, powdery appearance. And it appeared to be driven not by gravity, moving in concerted waves first this way, then that.

It in fact was neither powder nor sludge.

The black substance was composed of thousands of tiny, spindly-legged robots, each no more than a millimeter across. "Nanomites," the developers called them. They had been designed to infiltrate and break through any barriers—from bio-suits to air-filtered bunkers to hermetically sealed safe rooms or even submarines—that people might use to avoid the coming plague.

As the monkey struggled to free itself, the nanomite horde paused and seemed to orient itself to the creature, forming a wedge-shaped mass. And then it rushed across the laboratory floor.

The monkey managed to free an arm and swatted, once, twice, three times at the swarm gathering on its chest, but it was too late. The dark mound subsided as the little black creatures punched a hole through the safety fabric. The monkey's free arm shot out like it was giving a salute and then dropped limply. Its head likewise lolled onto its chest.

"One Missouri, two Missouri, three Missouri, four Missouri, five Missouri, six Missouri," said Victor Pierre aloud, just a trace of French accent to his voice. Then, before he got to the seventh Missouri, the monkey's body jolted, its faceplate going dark, as if a can of black spray paint had exploded inside.

Victor watched as the more easily digestible parts of the monkey's body were assimilated by the little creatures. They would soon replicate themselves. Doubling, tripling, quadrupling their number depending on the mass of their victim.

It was overkill, of course. Just one of the little black creatures had the mechanical means to burrow through conventional protective clothing, and each contained enough plague virus to touch off a pandemic all by itself. But he couldn't help but be pleased. Earth's purge was going to happen *so* much more quickly and efficiently than Ith's had.

"Commence full-scale production," he instructed his command feed as he pressed a button that filled the laboratory with an opaque cloud of sanitizing hydrofluoric acid.

The official time line for Earth's Reboot—from the release of the virus to the establishment of the first new city—was sixty days. Victor hoped to get this down to forty.

And things looked good to begin ahead of schedule. Like a rocket launch in its final countdown sequence, there were fewer and fewer opportunities for complications with every passing moment.

The chimeric rabbit had arrived just this week, it was true, and was proving to be surprisingly elusive. But they'd scaled up the response team, and the creature would shortly (and quietly) be intercepted.

Then there was the slightly more troubling Baltimore-DC situation. After hours of fruitless searching for a human or Mindthling agent (of roughly the same mass as Rex and his belongings: eighty-seven kilograms), an algorithm had belatedly spotted a Snapchat posted by a civilian aboard a MARC commuter train. The photograph corroborated nearly sixty witness reports of baby raccoons aboard the same commuter train.

It wasn't impossible for seven to twenty (reports varied significantly) wild creatures to make their way aboard a train. This wasn't, after all, Ith, where populations of wild animals either were fully under control or—where they weren't useful in the wider ecosystem—rendered entirely extinct. Coyotes, skunks, and raccoons, even sometimes bears and pumas, were not infrequent visitors in civilized areas of this Earth continent.

But creatures with communications hardware—particularly communications hardware that appeared to closely resemble a BNK-E strapped to their backs, as was the case with the specimen visible in the photo—*that* was not a frequent occurrence.

It was troubling that the creatures still hadn't been captured, but the situation was troubling on a wider level.

The hypothesis until now had had it that every outbound entity was to be replaced by an incoming *sentient creature that was (along with any possessions) of equivalent mass.*

But while it was known that *objects* could go along for the ride, nobody had ever posited that other *living things* might be numbered among these possessions.

Because it now seemed entirely possible that the mass of the striped creatures on the train—in total and including the device that at least one of them was wearing—was equivalent to Rex's Ith-bound mass.

And if that was the case, the entire scenario suggested a semi-sophisticated degree of knowledge on the part of the enemy.

Still, in the grand scheme, an antlered rabbit and some raccoons were not sixty-foot-tall reptilian monsters, nor poisonous oozing slimes. Both were threats chiefly on the level that they might manage to communicate to the local media and touch off a witch hunt for Victor and his fellow Deacons ahead of the planned initiation of the Purge in three days' time. It was a small concern, and one that could be gotten around by accelerating the operational timetable—if their cover became blown, they would simply launch the virus ahead of schedule. The dispersal wouldn't be as efficient—the nanomites hadn't yet been fully distributed and that would cause delays down the line—but the Purge would still work. The operational tipping point (the virus's successful incubation) had been achieved weeks ago. Rex wouldn't have left for Ith had it been otherwise.

The only other loose end, the old French woman now in Texas, was a similarly troubling non-risk. She'd hardly seemed a concern at all in the first assessment. She was, after all, nothing but an old lady from Earth. But the Ministry of Communications people had been wrong to downplay her media interest. She'd begun talking about her experience, speaking of big-eyed angels and a dark conspiracy that was taking place here on Earth. It all sounded too crackpot to take seriously, but more and more people were now flocking to see her, and the news cycle was beginning to pay attention.

It was a nice piece of luck that operatives had already been headed to Corpus Christi for the captured "giant squid"—the baby kraken. It was one of maybe only two Mindthlings left on this world, allowed to live only because of the transcense reserve it represented. But they'd stop and visit with the old French woman first. At her age, it wasn't at all unusual to have a stroke or heart attack. Especially after all the stress she'd been under lately.

PART III: PISMIRES

To understand that cleverness can lead to stupidity
is to be close to the ways of Heaven.

—HUANG BINHONG, *Insects and Flowers*
bcp §23¶1

CHAPTER 40

See No Evil

AS THE FINAL STEP OF THEIR INDUCTION INTO THE
Twelve, Rex had had Ith's Deacons' eyes surgically removed. It was a way of ensuring the dedication of his highest
administrators (for who would consent to have his or her eyes
put out for a cause in which they didn't fully believe?). It was
also a perfect symbol of the power and promise of Rex's new
world order. Little things like that did wonders among the seven
hundred million people of Ith to ensure an almost religious
faith in their leadership.

Of course Kempton Puber didn't know all the public relations reasons behind it. All he knew was that he'd never in
his life seen anything quite so hideous and unnerving as the

empty sockets in Deacon Sabrina Kim's face. Crimson scar tissue and what looked to be actual pieces of exposed bone were visible around the edges. Deep at the back of each misshapen crater—like undisturbed water at the bottom of a well— was a reflective silver screen. Kempton couldn't look away.

He had known the Deacons didn't have eyes, but he believed, as did all the regular citizens of Ith, that their sightlessness had been caused by the Minder himself. The story went that the Minder had so blessed their minds—in order that they could be the very best stewards of the world—that they no longer had need for common vision.

Kempton had only eaten a sesame kelp bar and three acai berries for breakfast, but it now seemed like too much. He trembled with the effort not to throw up even as he explained to himself that this must be some sort of rare privilege he was receiving.

In public and in all images and videos released to the public, the Deacons always wore robes, colored according to the ministry to which they were attached (green for INRI, brown for YSS, white for MuK, silver for MIM, azure for POP, gold for MA) with cowls keeping the upper parts of their faces—including their missing eyes—in shadow.

The Deacon acknowledged him now. He was transfixed by the furrowed, bone-ridged holes where her eyes had been. Something flashed in their depths—like light glinting on polished chrome. He didn't notice as she waved away her two attendants.

"Hello, Kempton Puber," she said. "I am Sabrina Kim."

"Your—your—your—"

"*Eminence* I think is the honorific," she said, smiling without showing any teeth.

"Your Eminence," he whispered.

"You've reviewed the script?" she said.

Kempton nodded, his head aching and his stomach churning. He somehow noticed she wasn't wearing a trace of makeup. He supposed there wasn't much point. She was so . . . Deacon Sabrina Kim was so . . . *hideous*.

"I understand you are an active participant in your student council," she said.

Kempton blinked and nodded as he replayed to himself what she'd just said.

"And so surely you have learned by now that diplomacy often requires that we not take the direct route to every result that we wish to obtain."

"Y-yes, Your E-eminence," he managed to say, fighting down his stupid revulsion. He'd known the Deacons had given up their eyes. It was the measure of their dedication. But all the pictures always had them wearing hoods. Had he thought they'd just have foreheads that ran seamlessly into their cheeks? Or that they'd wear sunglasses all the time?

"Good," replied Sabrina Kim. Kempton decided there was some sort of silvery material at the back of her sockets.

"Do you have any questions about what it is you're to do?"

"N-no, Your Eminence," said Kempton, deciding to focus his eyes on the wall behind her. The Twelve Tenets were listed in glimmering gold letters.

"Excellent. I understand you are already achieving some above-average scores in ARS 6D," she said.

Kempton nodded, surprised that she'd know such a thing and then realizing he shouldn't be surprised. The Deacons knew *everything*.

"Well, if you do well with your performance, perhaps we can speak to somebody over at the Abomination Redress Division about getting you niched. I understand they're about to become rather busy. Perhaps they could use your help."

Being an ARS (Abomination Redress Squad) officer was Kempton's dream career—killing monsters. He tried to say something appreciative but could only stammer, "R-r-r-really?"

"Be convincing," the eyeless woman replied. "This is a big moment, Kempton Puber. It's a *very* grownup thing you're about to do."

Kempton nodded as if he understood what that might mean.

"Ah, here's the cosmetics specialist," she said, as a long-legged man with a short torso came into the room.

"He'll take you to the green room and freshen you up before the recording. Remember, be convincing—really throw yourself into the role!"

Kempton nodded, his eyes lingering a moment on the Twelve Tenets. He figured Tenet Three, "Shun the sickness of uncertainty," and number Six, "Respect directives," were two he'd be observing shortly.

CHAPTER 41

The Short March

THE PLAN TO HIDE AMONG THE PRISONERS HAD seemed crazy to both Patrick and Oma. This was a world where every individual citizen was monitored by cameras, microphones, and tracking devices. But Ivan had been right. Ith's entire ultra-efficient penal system had been set up to minimize the effort and involvement of its managers. And belties weren't citizens. Belties were tools—cheap tools not exactly in short supply.

And the INRI officials in charge of the system probably weren't wrong to have embraced such a low-key strategy. Other than Ivan, no belty had ever successfully escaped the system. And why would anybody ever try to get *into* the system?

There were mechanisms in place to note accidental belty deaths. In addition to the watchful sky-eyes, the control computers kept meticulous records of the prisoners' comings and goings.

"The thing . . . with algorithms," Ivan said as they fell in with the work gang, "is they deal . . . with the data . . . they are given. . . . They don't go looking . . . for the data . . . they haven't . . . been given."

"Hey," said a wild-eyed man next to them, "what's the . . . dance beat all . . . the Deacons . . . are crazy for?!"

"I have no . . . idea, friend," said Ivan.

"The . . . Algo-Rhythm!"

It was among the worst jokes Patrick had ever heard, but the man was so clearly trying to make the best of his horrible situation that he made himself smile. Not that anybody could see him doing so, since nobody could turn their head on their own and the default head position when marching, of course, was straight ahead.

"See that . . . tower up . . . ahead?" asked Ivan.

Again Oma and Patrick refrained from nodding although they could see it plainly: atop the treeless hill they were approaching was a slender, needle-like shaft of gleaming aluminum, easily fifty stories high. Its top blossomed with an array of dishes, bulbs, and struts.

Ivan then explained, in his halting belty way, that the hill beneath the tower contained the broadcast bunker they needed to commandeer. As they got closer, Commonplace agents were going to set off a little explosion over to the east to draw away any nearby soldiers and drones. Also at that point, the

Deacons' surveillance systems would momentarily cut out, thanks to one of Ivan's viral hacks. And then Ivan explained what they needed to do.

Infiltrate and take over a high-tech military emplacement. All by themselves.

CHAPTER 42

A Chemist, a Librarian & an Eighth Grader

I **WAS KILLING MYSELF," SAID DAVE MURPHY, THE** man from the airplane, describing his former life as an FBI agent. "Working double shifts, triple shifts. Paperwork, field-work, busywork, forget about it."

"Did you nail lots of bad guys?" asked Neil from the back-seat. Dave was sitting up front in the taxi, next to the not-very-talkative driver. Both Dave and Uncle Andrew had been planning to rent cars, but they'd ended up having too much whiskey on the plane and so decided to share a cab since Dave's sister's place was near the Hampton Inn where Neil and Uncle Andrew were staying. But, first, because it was on the way,

Dave was going to show them the church where the miracle woman from France was making headlines.

"Bad guys? Yeah, I helped catch a few," said Dave. "But mostly it was staring at screens. Computer screens. Tablet screens. Conference screens. Smartphone screens. And then some super-unfun in-person meetings in between. And I guess some amount of driving around interviewing people. That part was fun."

"What kind of arrests did you make?" asked Neil.

"Tax cheats, money launderers, mostly. A couple drug dealers. I did work a serial killer case once."

"Did you get him?"

"Some agent from Nashville did. Mark Nichols, I think his name was. Guy's a legend."

"Oh," said Neil.

"Yeah, don't get ideas that Bureau work is all like a TV show or movie. For me, it was 70 percent perspiration, 28 percent office politics, and 2 percent existential crisis. In the end, it was that 2 percent that mattered most."

"What's an existential crisis?" asked Neil.

"It's picking up your head and asking yourself what the heck you're doing with yourself. It's like that Talking Heads song where the guy asks how he got there."

Neil was pretty sure his dad had more than once tried playing Talking Heads music for him, and he was pretty sure he hadn't liked it. Except maybe that "Psycho Killer" song. If that was them. That was a pretty funny song.

He caught a glimpse of himself in the taxi driver's rearview mirror and, though he knew he was smiling, he suddenly felt a little guilty about it. What was wrong with him, thinking about music when he was here to find out what was going on with his missing brother?

"Existential crisis, it's called?" he asked.

Dave and Uncle Andrew both nodded, and Neil nodded, too, repeating the expression inside his head so he wouldn't forget it. He'd definitely had this sensation before; just hadn't realized there was a name for it.

"Well, there it is," said Dave as they turned left onto a live oak–lined street. "There on the left.

"Sir," he said to the driver, "can you just pull over for a minute? We'll continue on to our destinations but we just want to get out and look around, okay?"

"Holy Comforter?" asked Neil, reading the sign as they pulled up across from the little stucco-walled chapel. "What's that? Like, a blanket?"

"I expect it's more like the concept of God's love," said Uncle Andrew.

"I think you're right on that score," said Dave. "It's got to be some kind of metaphor—barely big enough to fit a blanket in there."

The little stucco building with the lamb's-blood-red door was easily the smallest church Neil had ever seen. He figured the equipment shed for the pole-vault mats and stuff at his high school was probably a bit larger, although the equipment shed had never had quite such a line of people trying to get into it. People with folding chairs, sports umbrellas, camping rolls, coolers, and even an old man with a hibachi grill were lined up all the way down the block and around the corner and off to where he couldn't see.

The driver, wearing amber sunglasses, stared sullenly at Dave.

"You can keep the meter running," replied Dave.

"How far a walk is it to the hotel?" asked Uncle Andrew.

"Oh, just a few blocks—just back to the strip. Maybe ten minutes or something," said Dave.

"Well, why don't we just pay up and let this man go," said Uncle Andrew.

The driver sighed and jabbed a finger at the meter. It indicated twenty-six dollars.

"You take credit cards?" asked Uncle Andrew.

The driver now jabbed the same finger at a frayed, dirty Post-it somebody had taped to the dashboard. It read, "Credit card machine not working."

It looked like it had been there for years.

"I've got cash," said Dave.

"Oh, I do, too," said Uncle Andrew.

The two men tussled over the payment. It looked to Neil like they ended up splitting the cost, but he didn't care. He just wished they would both calm down and stop talking so much, and so loudly.

They exited the cab and stood next to the fire hydrant opposite the church.

The cab peeled away.

"Not the friendliest man, our driver," said Uncle Andrew.

"Total lizard," said Dave.

"Well, shall we—" said Uncle Andrew.

He was cut off by flashing lights behind and a megaphone squawk.

"Uh-oh," said Dave, smiling as he turned to see the police SUV that had pulled up behind them. "It's the piggly-wigglies!"

A woman's voice came over the loudspeaker: "PUT YOUR HANDS BEHIND YOUR HEADS AND NO SUDDEN MOVEMENTS!"

Instead of putting his hands behind his head—like Uncle Andrew and Neil quickly did—Dave slapped his knee as if this were one of the funnier things he'd ever heard. "This is too much!"

"What's going on, Dave?" asked Uncle Andrew.

"Buckle up, boys," said Dave as he flipped the bird at the police vehicle. "This is why they call this place Cop-Us Christi!"

CHAPTER 43
Antview

THE GROUND SHOOK BEFORE THEY HEARD THE BLAST,
shook so hard that almost everybody in the work gang
fell to the ground. Though it had taken place out of sight, past
some nearby hills, the blast had been powerful enough to
make the ground briefly turn to pudding.

"Holy—" said Patrick. "Was that the explosion you guys set
up as a *distraction*?"

Ivan ignored him. "Oma . . . the foil . . . hurry," he said as
his body and—with perfectly synched choreography—those
of all the other belties began to right themselves.

Oma took the folded sheet of lead foil and wrapped it around
the back of Ivan's collar. His legs immediately straightened,

causing him to fall on his back. And his hands began clapping again.

They were still at the back of the gang, and only one convict saw this happen—the woman who had tried to laugh.

"I knew you . . . guys seemed . . . different," she said as she stood and began to walk off past them. "Don't worry . . . I saw . . . nothing . . . nobody. . . . Nod's a wink . . . to a blind . . . Deacon."

"Take care . . . sister," said Ivan. "We hope . . . to free . . . you soon."

"Ha-ha . . . heh-heh," they heard her saying softly as she marched off.

A suitcase-sized drone buzzed over a nearby hill from the south.

"What do we—" Oma started to ask.

"Just . . . act naturally. . . . It's not . . . looking at us," said Ivan.

The machine hummed right over their heads and continued on to the north, soon disappearing over a ridge.

"Distraction . . . seems to . . . be working," said Ivan. "Now you . . . just need . . . to drag my . . . fat carcass . . . into cover . . . before it . . . wears off.

"I promise . . . I've been . . . dieting," he continued as Oma and Patrick started dragging him by his shoulders. "Other than . . . Seth's . . . soda."

Ivan wasn't quite obese, but he weighed a bit more than the two of them put together, and both kids were pretty exhausted and sore by the time they got him to a stand of old cedar trees.

"This looks . . . plenty . . . comfortable," said Ivan of the peaty ground.

"Do you want us to stand you up?" asked Patrick.

"No, I . . . like looking . . . up through . . . trees, don't . . . you?"

Oma and Patrick both looked up through the cathedral ceiling of evergreen branches above them.

"Makes me feel small," said Patrick.

"Exactly," said Ivan. "It is . . . good to . . . see the . . . world as . . . an ant . . . from time . . . to time."

Ivan then instructed Oma and Patrick to roll him on his side and place his binky on his face so that he could talk them through getting past the bunker's security.

Then he told them to put their skin-suits back on.

Patrick and Oma both groaned. They of course weren't thrilled with the bright-green prison suits they'd been wearing, but at least they weren't skintight and useless against the cold.

"Do we have to?" asked Oma. But she knew there was no arguing. She and Patrick went off to change behind separate trees.

CHAPTER 44

Bad Noises

BUNBUN PEERED UP OVER THE EDGE OF THE SUBWAY
platform where he was still hiding, waiting for the next
train. He'd decided it was best to reverse course and duck back
into the tunnel after the incident with the conductor with the
camera. He knew time was of the essence, but on the other
hand he'd clearly made good progress. He'd started his tunnel
journey above 190th Street and the tiled letters on the wall
said this was 81st Street, almost all of the way to his 50th
Street destination.

"American Museum of Natural History?" he said to himself, reading aloud the rest of the sign. What was that supposed
to mean? A history museum might make sense—containing

artifacts, inventions, and battle scenes, et cetera. And a nature museum—cataloging species of animals and plants—certainly could be a thing. But animals and plants didn't write histories and humans hadn't even been around except in the past couple hundred thousand years. Nature had been around for billions.

He shrugged. It didn't really matter. What mattered was that he get someplace whcre a lot of people would see him, and that he then do a good job on his big speech. He rehearsed it once again.

"People of Earth, please lend me your eyes and, especially, your generous ears. I realize," he muttered to himself, "you may be a little surprised to see a strange talking creature like myself in your midst, but please pay attention to my words here, and to every letter they contain. There is grave peril in your midst. There are men and women among you who are no longer men and women. Many of them work for a company called Kingaroo, and most often they go by two first names. Now, this is not to say that all people with two first names, nor even all people who work for Kingaroo, are evil-doers. I mention it only to help channel your attention toward those who mean you harm.

"Please open your eyes and ask why they have been working on secret technologies to spy on you, to strengthen themselves, and—most important—*to kill most all of you.*

"For that is what they are planning—they mean to wipe out civilization and start again, start again according to their own selfish plan. They have engineered a virus, a virus for which I have been given the formula—a formula that, as I will explain, is contained in the very letters of the words I am now saying—"

BunBun heard a squeal and peeked up over the platform again. A stroller-bound child was protesting to her father, arching her back. "Triceratops *again!*" she said rather insistently.

The father smiled and proffered a slice of apple that didn't appeal at all to the child but made BunBun's stomach growl. He hadn't had a proper meal in over a day, not since he'd raided that grocery store dumpster in Yonkers and found a couple cabbages.

The high-pitched ting of a train's metal wheels upon the steel tracks brought BunBun's wits back to him, but not before he noticed a man in a black suit and sunglasses up on the platform. He was staring at a smartphone that looked suspiciously like a binky. He was sweeping it back and forth as he walked, advancing like a night watchman with a flashlight.

The man's mouth moved, as if he were talking to himself, and BunBun heard—even through the approaching cacophony of the oncoming train—amplified voices coming from the southern tunnel, past the platform.

This was not good. This was *so* not good. The man on the platform was walking faster toward him now.

BunBun ducked as far as he could under the ledge of the platform, huddling in a shallow pile of dirty food wrappers, empty plastic bottles, and paper coffee cups. If the man got to the end of the platform first, before the train came up, and looked over the ledge . . .

BunBun could no longer see up onto the platform, of course,

but he had a good view down the tracks to the south. He noticed the weak bluish light of a portable screen emerging from the south tunnel. And then another light appeared. And another. He tried to slow his breathing and heart rate. He had to remain very still so their sensors wouldn't find him. And now the source of the light moved out of the tunnel and into view. It was a woman holding a binky and wearing the same sort of jumpsuit the man in the cemetery had been wearing this morning, the man with the drone. He could recognize the virus logo on her baseball cap even from this distance.

She stopped stock-still, in complete counterpoint to BunBun's own heart, which seemed eager to climb up and out his throat, and signaled to the other lights behind her in the tunnel. Then she brought her other hand down in a dead point, right at BunBun.

With a quick look up the north tunnel to ensure he wasn't going to be overtaken by the train (it sounded like it was almost upon him but was still a good fifty meters away) he leapt from the garbage pile, out into the middle of the tracks, and up onto the passenger platform.

Shouts and screams greeted him, and the apple-refusing child in the stroller squealed with delight. Her startled father and a half-dozen green-wearing tourists all jumped with surprise. The angry-looking man in the suit might have been startled but didn't let on. BunBun paused a moment to say, "Leave me alone and I'll leave you alone, okay?"

The man reached for something inside his jacket, something BunBun assumed was a weapon, so he lifted himself up on one leg and delivered a powerful kick straight into the center of the man's chest. The man pinwheeled backward into the wall and his head smacked against the tiles.

He slumped to the floor.

"Sorry about that," said BunBun. He looked around and noticed the father of the child had dropped his bag of apple slices onto the platform's cement floor. He took a quick bound, picked them up, and offered them back.

"Nn-nno," said the man.

"May I have them, in that case?" asked BunBun.

"Puh-pul-lease," begged the man.

The child stared up at the giant jackalope with glowing fascination.

"Thank you very much. I'll repay you for this kindness, I promise," BunBun said, quickly scarfing down the apples.

"Mmm, so good," he mumbled.

"You're a fat deer!" said the child suddenly.

"Actually," said BunBun, more than a little mortified by the comment, "I'm—"

He broke off—the female agent from the south tunnel had made it up onto the far end of the platform and was stalking his way.

"Thanks again," said BunBun as he bounded into the nearby museum entryway.

CHAPTER 45
Bunker Bunkum

FOUR, THREE . . . ONE," IVAN SAID THROUGH THE earpieces of their skin-suits.

The huge metal door was set deep in the base of the perfectly round hill, the path to it bulwarked by three-foot-thick concrete walls.

"Umm," said Oma.

"Anything . . . happen?" asked Ivan.

"N-no," said Patrick.

"Frag . . . nabbit," said Ivan, "I must . . . have jimmied . . . the wrong . . . cipher. . . . Hang on. . . . How about . . . *now?*"

"Umm," said Oma.

"Nn—" Patrick started to say, but then there was a *thunk,*

followed by a low mechanical rumble as the door slid away to their left.

"You got it," Patrick corrected himself.

"Don't worry— . . . probably . . . the standard . . . video . . . and holo- . . . feeds . . . will be . . . playing, but . . . the sentry . . . system . . . should be . . . offline."

"Okay," said Oma as she and Patrick stepped across the door's track into the bunker. "How can we tell the sentry system is off?"

"No poison . . . gas? . . . Electrified . . . floors? . . . Guard dogs?" asked Ivan.

"Um, no," confirmed Patrick.

"Then we're . . . okay," affirmed Ivan. "Main hall . . . will come . . . to a T. . . . Should be . . . an elevator. . . . Go down two . . . levels. . . . Go right . . . first left then . . . second right. . . . Broadcast studio . . . will be on your, . . . let's see, . . . left."

"Okay," said Patrick, looking over at Oma. "Are we going to remember that?"

Oma nodded and gave him a thumbs-up. "Straight, elevator down, go right, first left, second right, studio on left."

Ivan had already warned them that their connection was likely to be severed once they were inside the fortified hill. The radio waves couldn't penetrate the soil, concrete, and metal of the subterranean bunker, and patching a signal through the comm system would be very difficult.

"I've downloaded . . . the floor plan . . . onto your . . . binkies as . . . well."

"And, if we don't understand anything, we just come back up, right?" asked Oma.

"Yes, but . . . try not to. . . . We probably . . . have . . . only a . . . couple deuces . . . before somebody . . . notices."

Once again Patrick had forgotten how long a deuce was. He supposed he could have looked it up on his binky, but didn't want to discover that it was much less than the twenty minutes he assumed it was.

There was no point worrying about it anyhow. One of the last *Commonplace* entries My-Chale had quoted had been along the lines of how courage is a sandcastle and overthinking the incoming tide.

"No problem!" he said, and tried to believe it.

"Good luck . . . you two," Ivan's voice crackled.

"This is like something from a video game," said Patrick. The corridor they were walking down reminded him acutely of some of the levels in Halo or one of those other sci-fi first-person-shooter games Neil played endlessly. Every surface was perfectly formed and shone as if it had been rendered by a computer and extruded from a 3D printer.

And many of the surfaces weren't merely surfaces but also screens. Numbers, sports scores, weather and news reports displayed upon the surfaces and, in some cases, in front of or above them, as holographs, like the half-sized, heavily made-up, heavily coiffed weather forecaster who suddenly appeared in front of them.

"Jeez," said Patrick. "I thought she was real for a sec."

"What's a sec?" asked Oma.

"Short for a—never mind. I meant, like, for a quint," explained Patrick, catching his breath.

"We shouldn't worry that all these are playing, should we?"

asked Patrick. "That it doesn't mean they're working through Ivan's hack?"

"This is pretty standard null-state, screen-saver stuff. I think if they'd worked through the hack, we'd know about it. What did Ivan say? Collared bears and poison gas?"

"I guess that's right," agreed Patrick.

They stopped and watched the holographic woman silently speaking and gesturing at the cloud-swirling map on the hallway wall. Rays of sun, temperatures, and a bunch of other symbols moved about as she gestured.

"Looks like we have some nice weather headed our way. Let's get moving so we can live to enjoy it, shall we?" said Oma, sticking a finger through one of the woman's eyes.

Patrick smiled and nodded. "Yeah, let's go. There's the elevator. We take it down to C4, right?"

"C2," replied Oma, holding up the map on her binky.

Patrick was about to say something about how at least he got the letter right when all the screens synched to the same scene: a huge parade ground, overflowing with concentrically arranged, uniformed government employees.

At the center, a small figure flanked by two imposing, goggle-wearing soldiers stood upon a dais.

The small figure grew as the camera zoomed in, and his holograph shortly inhabited the floor right in front of Patrick and Oma.

They both stopped stock-still and gasped.

It was Kempton. And he was crying.

CHAPTER 46

General Admission, General Alarm

THE GRIFFINS, NANA, AND MR. COFFIN HAD A FINE ride on the shuttle, but the A Train was shut down because of a police incident uptown, so they decided to abandon the subway.

They ended up taking three cabs. Nana, Lucie, and the Twins took one; Rick, Eva, and Carly took another; and Mr. Coffin rode in the third cab with Mary, who asked him to retell his "home invasion" story.

She found his experience interesting for three reasons. First, it pretty much confirmed that this Mr. BunBun her children had met had been in her next-door neighbor's house at roughly the same time as Patrick's disappearance. Which underscored the fact that BunBun was directly involved.

Second, Coffin's insistence that BunBun was actually a man in costume bolstered her increasing confidence that Bun-Bun was not human. Her old neighbor said more than once that it was "a very, very realistic costume," and that it was "obviously worn to disguise identity," but it didn't make any sense. Why would somebody go to the length of an elaborate jackalope costume just to drown a person's phones, leave a couple weird notes, and then ransack their bird feeders?

Third, the notes confirmed for Mary that they were dealing with a wider supernatural phenomenon here. Mr. Coffin said the notes BunBun had left him were on business cards that read, "Trans-World Consultant and Fomenter." And he said that this BunBun's visit had been accompanied by the distinct smell of church incense. Just as she had found after Patrick's disappearance.

She didn't know what to do with all this information yet, but she was reassured that bringing the family to New York had been the right thing to do.

She still didn't much care for Mr. Coffin. He spoke in an affected lockjaw tone, like that Buckley man who used to be on television. And he seemed to have a generally snobby, old-fashioned view of the world. He kept speaking of "criminal elements" and saying how society seemed to be "in decline" and "morally adrift." He also said that "the art of parenting" had been "entirely forgotten," and Mary had the distinct sense that she herself was included in this generalization.

Exiting the cab in front of the museum, Nana was quick to sense the awkwardness between them and came to the rescue.

"So, what do you do with yourself, Mr. Coffin?" she asked as the old man followed Mary up the stone steps to the museum entrance.

"Why, I'm retired," he said.

"But you're so young," she said to him.

"Oh, w-well," he stammered as he noted what seemed to him to be a flirtatious twinkle in her eye.

"Really, though," she said, repeating her question as they walked up the steps to catch up with the rest of the family, "what do you do with yourself? You seem like a vital personality. Do you have any hobbies? Causes you support?"

"Ah, well, I am on the board of the Van der Hook Historical Society," he said. "And I attend a fund-raising dinner for the Choral Arts Society of Bedford."

"I knew it," said Nana. "Virile men like you must always stay in motion."

Mr. Coffin didn't even try to find words to reply to this comment. He simply beamed.

"You guys have a nice ride?" asked Rick as the family reached the top of the stairs. He was steadfastly resisting the Twins' efforts to pull him inside their beloved museum.

"Just fine," said Mary as they filed into the cathedral-like museum lobby dominated by a towering apatosaurus skeleton.

"Kids!" said Mary to Lucie, Eva, and Carly—the Twins knew the drill and had already grabbed their badges. "Come get your passes!"

But before anybody responded, a wailing alarm went off and an emergency strobe began to flash.

And a moment later a large antlered rabbit bounded out of the Hall of North American Mammals and—as the crowd began to scream—hurried out the Central Park West exit.

CHAPTER 47
Feed Kill

THEY KNEW THEY DIDN'T HAVE TIME TO STOP AND watch Kempton's speech, but they did it anyway. This was Oma's brother. And, in the background video frame unfolding on the wall behind Kempton, they also watched her parents being handcuffed and put inside an armored INRI paddy wagon.

Patrick put his hand out for Oma to hold, but instead she gripped his forearm and proceeded to dig her fingers into it. It was a little painful but he didn't complain. This was so crazy. Kempton and his family were being accused of conspiring with the Anarchists to undermine productivity and progress. And Kempton was saying that he, Patrick, was *not* an actual

Earthling; he was a genetically engineered aberration the enemy had created as part of a sickening attempt to impair the Minder's vision.

As Kempton's fake confession ended, Oma abruptly let go of Patrick's arm, rubbed her eyes, and—with a quick glance at her binky—rushed into the elevator.

"Hurry!" she said to Patrick.

"Are you okay? I mean, it looks like they're locking up your family," Patrick said as he joined her.

"I don't know what to think," she said as she pressed the C2 button and the doors closed. "It's obviously all staged, but if the Kempton I know is falsely confessing to a crime against the state, then—yes, he and my mother and father are probably in serious trouble. Probably they'll put them all in collars."

"But," she continued, talking fast, "even if it's all my fault, what can we do about it now? Would going and turning ourselves in to the Deacons help any? Would they suddenly be, like, 'Well, thank you. Here—we'll let your family go and we'll stop oppressing the people of Ith and killing Mindthlings and everything will be awesome!'?"

"Probably not," said Patrick, shaking his head sympathetically.

"And probably they're doing it not just to undermine your status, but to get at me. And obviously they just did: like a couple of idiots, we just blew at least five terts watching their little show, which means we have five terts less to get this mission done with and get out of here alive."

"You don't think they know we're here already? I mean, doesn't it seem awfully coincidental that this happened just now—"

"That's just what I was checking. No, if they knew we were here, like Ivan said with the sentinels and whatnot, we'd know it."

She showed him the screen of her binky. "Here, look." It was playing the same broadcast in miniature. "It's a full-network feed, just like what we're trying to get out here ourselves."

The elevator came to a stop, and they emerged into another hallway. The walls were occupied by newscasters dissecting the implications of Kempton's speech and also discussing a massive military mission to locate Patrick and the enemy leadership. As he and Oma hurried down the passage to the left, they heard one of the broadcasters say that in three days, on Sevensday—the first day of the New Year—the Seer would address the world and lay out a five-point plan to finally rid humanity of the Anarchist menace.

"These guys are giving me a headache," said Patrick as he followed Oma down the second corridor to the right.

"So try turning them off," said Oma.

"What?" said Patrick.

"Kill feed!" said Oma. The walls immediately stopped playing the news and displayed a scene from a sunlit meadow.

"Much better," said Patrick as they spied the studio and hurried inside.

"So," said Patrick as the doors closed behind them, "will everybody now think I'm a fake? I mean, they've basically told everybody I'm an agent of the Anarchists, versus being an emissary of the Minder. Should we just turn around and go back to Ivan? If I do this broadcast now—"

"Look," she said. "You *have* gone missing, right? Sooner or later, they were going to have to say something. Explain where you are. And, yes, I'm sure this way they do slightly have their butts covered in case you are ever seen in public again and tell a different story. But you have more to say here than just claiming to really be a human from Earth and not some sort of weird sci-fi genetic experiment."

"You mean, telling everybody Rex is back."

"And the other things we discussed, too. The ruined cities out there that prove we weren't living like cavemen fifty years ago. The collar camps filled with people who have dared to speak their own minds. The secret surveillance all around. And, now, the fact that Kempton and my parents are being framed."

"You still think it can work?"

"You get on the worldwide feed and, yes, there's a very good chance you'll get people doing that thing the Deacons hate most."

"Asking questions?" said Patrick.

Oma smiled and touched the tip of his nose. "It's something."

"Speaking of questions," said Patrick. "Why is there absolutely nobody in this bunker?"

"Ivan explained this to us—don't you remember? It's a failsafe the Deacons put in place just in case there was a problem with their central system. If we were able to blow out the main broadcast center in Silicon City, for instance, they have a bunch of these stations set up around the world that they could use for backup. They're big on redundancies."

"Okay, so what next?" said Patrick, taking note of the sound stage, control booth, and some rather enormous turret-mounted cameras around them.

"Just get up on the stage and do your speech," said Oma.

"You sure you know how to run all this?" asked Patrick.

Oma gestured at her binky and was starting to speak when suddenly the cameras came to life and wheeled around to focus on them.

"What's going on?" asked Patrick. "Did you turn on the—"

A voice behind them interrupted.

"That was all me, actually," said a mellifluous voice.

"No . . . ," said Oma.

"Way," finished Patrick, regarding the imposing man in the black turtleneck.

"Yes way," replied Rex.

CHAPTER 48
Hostile Boarders

THE NUMBATS HUDDLED SAFELY INSIDE THE CABIN of a small recreational fishing boat, *China Muldoon*, docked in a marina on the western bank of the Anacostia River.

They'd ended up coming ashore in a small yacht club and quickly hidden themselves inside this unoccupied motorboat, sneaking in through a cloth-covered vent above the main cabin door. And then burrowed beneath the bunk cushions in the cabin under the foredeck.

Around five thirty in the afternoon, Trixy announced something was wrong.

"Yeah," said Barb, "Shifty's giving the speech in her sleep again."

Trixy could hear her sister muttering the message softly, the part at the end where they explain to everybody how to extract the code from what they've just said. "And, now, take each of the letters of the words I've said up to this point and find the *A*s, the *U*s, the *C*s, and the *G*s, and put them down in exact order, and you'll have the genetic code for the vaccine, the vaccine to save you all!"

"That's so annoying," said Trixy, who, like the rest of them, had rehearsed the thing a bazillion times already, "but, no, I'm talking *seriously* wrong. Here, *look* at this." She nodded at the binky screen strapped to Shorty's slumbering back.

"You see the time code on our cloaking program there?"

Barb saw a bunch of weird boxes and numbers up in the corner of the map on her sister's screen. None of it made much sense to her. She shrugged.

"It's stopped counting. It's supposed to wink out entirely if it's been compromised—if Rex's people have disabled it—but I don't remember anything about it *stopping* and just staying there."

"Maybe it's broken," said Barb.

"Or maybe they broke it and are trying to make us think it's still running. Either way, I think it's time we said goodbye to our binky. We should be okay without it from here anyhow. I think I know the best place for us to go."

"You *think* you know?" said Barb.

"There's this place called the Capitol Building—"

"Wait, didn't you say this whole city was the capital?"

"Right, but *this* is the Capitol *Building*, it's like the center of the whole place. It's the source of hundreds of mass transmissions every day. Transmissions that reach millions of people around the world."

Just as BunBun had used his binky to study New York's geography and media patterns, Trixy had spent the past two days studying Washington, DC, looking for the very best spots from which to warn the world.

"Yeah, you can't do anything there without making news, but it's a tough approach. Lots of small streets between here and there, lots of surveillance cameras through which Rex's Deacons-in-training might spot us.

"Although," she continued, "I have some backup locations in mind, too, like the White House, the National Mall—and there's a lot of outdoor population density and personal device broadcasts up in the area called Northwest—"

Barb looked at her glassily.

"But let's wake Shorty up and dump this device in the river right now. We knew we might have to go offline before very long. And let's get some breakfast—the sun'll be back down shortly and, like I was saying, we shouldn't be dawdling here—"

"What's that noise?" whispered Sven from the far end of the forward V-shaped bunk.

"Shhhh!" said Trixy, which woke up Shorty, Levanty, and everybody who wasn't already up.

"Footsteps!" whispered Trixy, hastily turning off the binky and undoing Shorty's straps.

"Great!" whispered Barb sarcastically.

"What's happening?" said Shorty.

"We have company," said Sven.

"Shh!" insisted Trixy. The footsteps had stopped, and there was a strange high-pitched electronic sound.

Then there was a man's voice, just a brief word they couldn't make out. And then the boat rocked slightly. There were more footsteps at the back of the boat—one, two, three, four pairs of feet, at least, and then somebody rattling the lock on the cabin door.

"Listen, we need to get out of here. Let's climb out the little window there," Trixy whispered, clambering up the bunk and undoing the hasp on the little portal. "As soon as you land in the river"—Barb groaned, but Trixy either didn't hear or simply ignored it—"dive as deep as you can, dive and swim with the current—there's another bridge—"

BANG!

Somebody had just delivered a mighty blow to the cabin door. Bright light filled the galley at the back of the boat. Like trained acrobats, the nine numbats climbed up over each other and out through the open portal, plunging almost silently into the river.

Moments later, four armed commandos stormed into the cabin cruiser's forward cabin and found nothing but an electronic device slightly more high-tech than anything that had ever been sold in an Earth store, along with a little belted harness, just about the right size for a beagle, or an above-average-sized marsupial anteater.

CHAPTER 49
Expedient Exigencies

VICTOR PIERRE WAS NOT PLEASED THAT THE enemy Mindthling, the rabbit chimera, had escaped the subway tunnel. It would have been so easy to end it there.

On the other hand, he wasn't exactly panicked. Over a hundred Homeland Security personnel and special operatives were descending on the scene, including a helicopter. The backstory for the federal agencies and the police was that a Department of Defense genetic project had gone terribly awry and this was a mop-up operation.

Which would doubtless keep them quiet. As to civilian discovery, since this was all taking place in the center of one of the biggest cities in the world, the immediate area had to be taken off the network, blacked out. And anybody with special interest in the scene, anybody who came into contact with the creature, would have to be interdicted and dealt with. And the story would need to be set straight.

That of course included the family of the boy. The family that had somehow managed to end up in this very place at this very time. Clearly they could not be allowed to continue to do whatever it was they thought they were doing.

The cover-up wouldn't need to be too elaborate. In less than twenty-three dunts, the Purge would begin. The virus and the nanomites would be released all around the world. March 20, forty years to the day after Ith's Purge began, this world, too, would be reborn.

The element of risk—even the *chance* somebody might be able to derail the operation—was already minuscule. Rex wouldn't have gone back to Ith already if he hadn't been confident that the course was set.

Still, this line of thinking reminded him that his absent leader was always mindful of contingencies and that he had another mission for Victor to accomplish, depending on what transpired in the next hour. Rex had instructed him that if two days went by without another messenger arriving from Ith, Victor was to execute a backup plan with regard to the Griffin family.

Rex had left just enough transcense to accomplish the task.

CHAPTER 50

Friends on the Force

BABY, YOU'RE LOOKING GREAT!" DAVE SHOUTED AT the policewoman.

"That's probably not too smart," Uncle Andrew muttered to Neil. Both already had their hands behind their heads but Dave was sauntering toward the gun-drawn policewoman as if approaching a relative.

"You take one step closer, sir, and—"

"We can hug?" said Dave, pausing but inching his leg forward and shifting his weight so that he actually would be taking that one step closer and—

"Oh, I *guess*," said the woman, holstering her gun and rushing forward, practically tackling Dave.

It dawned on Neil and Uncle Andrew that Dave and the officer knew each other, and apparently quite well. Still, they kept their hands locked behind their heads as the woman had instructed.

"At ease, soldiers," she said as she and Dave ended their bear hug, and then added, "And are you going to introduce us, big brother?"

"Andrew, Neil, this is Officer Babette Murphy of the CCPD. Officer Murphy, this is Andrew Meyer and his nephew Neil Griffin, visiting Corpus Christi on an investigation involving the Miracle Woman."

"Is that so?" said Officer Murphy. "Official business? You're not just regular religious pilgrims like the rest of 'em?" she said, gesturing at the people camped up and down the sidewalk in front of the church. "Don't have some infirmities you want fixed up? Have her bless your cell phone so you can do better at fantasy sports?"

"Get out!" said Dave. "Nobody has their cell phone—"

"Well, not at this church they won't, actually. She's asked that nobody bring any electronics inside the chapel. You've got to leave anything that runs on batteries outside with an attendant."

Uncle Andrew raised an eyebrow.

"But there was a man here this morning," said Officer Murphy, "trying to get his fishing rod blessed."

"People are so special," said Dave.

"So, what's the situation?" asked Officer Murphy.

"Umm," said Uncle Andrew. "We really, actually . . . I know it sounds crazy but we have a relative who was involved with circumstances that sound very similar to this Miracle Woman's."

"Clouds of holy smoke and divine teleportations?"

"Something like that," said Neil.

"And corporate-government conspiracies," added Dave.

"Well, that part I can savvy," said Officer Murphy. "You wouldn't believe the flak we've been getting from the Feds about this operation. The sheriff's about to dump a drum of hurt all over the G-men who've come to town in the past twenty-four hours. What a bunch of weenies—I can't believe you ever worked in DC, brother."

"Is it the Bureau?" Dave asked.

"The ones driving us crazy say they're with Homeland Security. Between them and this Kingaroo outfit—"

"Kingaroo?" asked Uncle Andrew.

She nodded down the block. A small truck with a cherry-picker crane on its back was parked at the corner inside a small phalanx of orange road cones.

"Just showed up. Apparently every comm tower in the county suddenly needs updating."

"Oh, wow," said Uncle Andrew.

"So," said Officer Murphy, "what's the story with this relative of yours? You said a similar situation with Madame Carruth here? Holed up in a church in a foreign land or what?"

"My brother disappeared," said Neil, getting tired of everybody beating around the bush. "And it smelled like incense where he disappeared. *And* he called us from France but now there's no record of his having called."

"And guess what company is the biggest international

telecom infrastructure provider in the world right now," said Uncle Andrew, nodding down the street at the Kingaroo truck.

"Well," said Officer Murphy, taking all this in and working her jaw as she thought something through. "As some president once said, the enemy of my pain in the butt is my friend . . . you guys want to go in and meet Lilian?"

"Lilian?" asked Andrew.

"The Miracle Woman," said Officer Murphy. "She and I are practically on a first name basis at this point."

"She calls you 'Baby'?" asked Dave.

"You, darling brother, are the only human I let call me that. No, she prefers to call me Babette—a good French name, after all."

"You're serious," said Uncle Andrew. "What about this line of people?"

"I think Lilian will take more of an interest in your missing nephew than in the next blessing of the hunting rifle or lottery ticket that's coming her way."

"Well, thank you, Off—"

"You can call me Babette, too," she said, giving Uncle Andrew a wink. "At least provided none of my fellow officers are around."

"Yeah, Baby!" said Dave.

Neil rolled his eyes and wondered how adults always managed to be so awkward.

CHAPTER 51
Central Park Steeplechase

IT WAS CLEAR FROM THE START THAT THEY WERE going to have to split up. The Twins and Mr. Coffin simply couldn't move very fast.

After the briefest discussion between Mary and her mother, it was decided that Nana would stay back with the children and Mr. Coffin. Obviously they couldn't just leave the three of them unattended. Meantime, Rick, Lucie, Eva, and Carly followed after Mary, pursuing the fleeing shape of BunBun past screaming, shouting, and generally freaking-out pedestrians into the trees, paths, fields, and old stoneworks of Central Park.

The rabbit from another world had a good head start,

however, and was a significantly better cross-country runner than the Griffins. Even Mary, who ran four miles a day, rain or shine, quickly realized there was no way she could keep up. They'd not made it a dozen yards into the park when she entirely lost sight of him, bounding up and over a chain-link fence they couldn't possibly scale.

"I think he's heading south," said Mary, gesturing to the path to their right. It was west of his course but led downtown, parallel to Central Park West. "If we're right about him wanting to get to Rockefeller Center or Times Square, he's going to get down to the Lake and have to come back our way, or go around the other side. Either way, he'll have to come west and maybe we can cut the corner on him before he leaves the park."

It made passing sense to the rest of them, and they were already too out of breath and excited to argue otherwise.

A number of green-wearing St. Patrick's Day tourists ran toward them out of the park, clearly away from the large animal they'd just seen.

"There's an escaped bear!" said a bearded young dude in a tweed jacket and green sweater, stopping as the Griffins forged ahead into the park.

The side path led them through a brick-walled tunnel, alongside a carriage path, past park benches, around joggers, in-line skaters, strollers, and more green-clad tourists. None of these people had seen BunBun, and they were merely surprised and curious at the sight of a family running as helter-skelter as they were, and not in exercise clothing.

Soon they could glimpse the body of water known simply

as the Lake. Leaving Strawberry Fields to their right, they crossed West Drive and ran along the shoreline.

The sound of bagpipes—perhaps players warming up for the parade—could be heard in the distance. But they were soon drowned out by police sirens and the approaching whumps of a helicopter.

"He's got to be over there," said Mary. She, swimmer Eva, and soccer star Carly had enough breath to speak, but Lucie and Rick were panting badly.

The helicopter was close now, low enough to froth the surface of the Lake. A cloud of wavelet-spawned mist billowed around the edges of the downdraft and dampened them all.

The *thud-thud-thud* of its rotors sounded like a giant beating a stadium-sized rug with a telephone pole. Two black vans screamed down West Drive just then, blue lights flashing like they were part of a diplomatic convoy.

Mary stopped suddenly and led Carly and Eva to the side of the Lake for a better look. In the water, something was causing a subtle V-shaped wake ahead of the approaching black helicopter. It looked like the surface of the pool just after a swimmer has kick-turned and before they break the surface—

"There he is!!" shouted Carly as the rest of the family caught up.

"He was swimming underwater!" said Mary as his distinctive antlers and the waterlogged brown fur of his back appeared. He'd reached the shallows now and was bounding sluggishly across the muddy inlet, heading for the far corner of Wagner Cove, directly south of where they stood.

The helicopter quickly overtook him, and the big rabbit

stopped suddenly, putting his paws to his ears and looking upward, where a man dressed in a black tactical uniform was leaning out on the landing rail with a scope-mounted rifle. As they looked on, the gun issued a puff of smoke, and BunBun jolted, a slim, red-feathered silver dart suddenly sticking from the side of his neck.

Meanwhile, a half-dozen helmet-wearing men dressed like SWAT team specialists sprinted into the shallow water and grabbed the collapsing rabbit.

A middle-aged man carrying bagpipes ahead of them on the path started yelling at the men. Only every other word he said was audible as the helicopter turned and flew back across the Lake, but he was obviously very angry.

As the men dragged BunBun to a black van waiting on the southern shore, the man stomped his foot, tucked his instrument into position, put his pipe in his mouth, and began to play a song that Rick and Lucie (the one child Rick had ever been able to truly bond with over music, though in recent years she was largely listening to her own stuff) recognized as the Clash's "I Fought the Law." He only kept it up for a few bars, however, because two black-clad men wearing helmets and bulletproof vests came up and put him in handcuffs.

"Oh, no!" shouted Mary, already turning to get back on the path.

Rick grabbed her shoulder. "And look down there!"

Other men and women in black were accosting joggers, cyclists, and pedestrians down near the end of the Lake, pushing them down to the ground and taking their cell phones and cameras.

"We need to get out of here. Did any of you snap any pictures of that?"

"My phone won't even turn on," said Eva.

They realized, as they hurried through the bushes toward Central Park West, that none of their phones was working. It was black screens all around.

CHAPTER 52

See You Later, Transubstantiator

HE'S A HOLOGRAPH!" SAID OMA.

"Flesh is overrated," said Rex.

"But he's talking to us—he knows we're here!" said Patrick.

"Listen," said Rex. "Since that's evidently true—I can see and hear you, and you can see and hear me—why don't we talk? Maybe we can help each other."

"He's trying to distract us," said Oma. "If he could stop us he would!"

"Can't we just talk? Isn't that the polite thing to do when you first meet somebody? As opposed to running away."

"You're right," Patrick said to Oma, ignoring Rex.

"He must be coming through the communication systems but not have control of the security. That's why we aren't being locked in here." Oma gestured at the still-open studio door.

"I would never try to impede your progress," said Rex.

"Should we still try to do the video—" Patrick started to say but caught himself. Clearly, if Rex was controlling the cameras in here, they were going to have trouble filming and putting out a feed.

"Why don't you two have a seat?" said Rex, smiling with his perfect teeth. "There's a lot you don't know about what's going on, and I think—"

"Kill feed!" yelled Oma, but Rex's holograph didn't go away. In fact, it stepped toward them.

"Really now," he continued. "We haven't even met and you seem to be judging me without even having—"

"He must be breaking through the hack—seriously, let's get out of here before he manages to take back over the entire place!" shouted Oma.

Patrick, who had been arriving at the same conclusion himself, didn't need to be told twice. He ran out after her into the hallway, where, predictably, Rex's holograph rematerialized.

"Seriously, can't we just introduce ourselves? Hi," he said, smirking and extending an elbow. He'd long ago taught the people of Ith to bump clothed elbows rather than shake hands, as a means to curtail the exchange of germs. "I'm Rex. Rex Abraham."

Fortunately Oma had a better sense of direction than Patrick did and got them back to the elevator without any bad turns.

It was still there waiting with its doors open.

"Be my guest," said Rex with a smirk. "It's still working. After a fashion."

Patrick and Oma exchanged a look.

"Are there stairs?" asked Patrick.

"Stairs?" Oma asked.

"Patrick's used to stairs inside buildings," Rex said. "Earth's elevators aren't quite as reliable as they are here. Present situation excepted, of course."

"He's bluffing about the elevator," said Oma, stepping inside. "And what choice do we have, anyhow?"

"That's true," said Rex.

"G Level!" shouted Oma as Patrick followed her inside. The compartment closed and they felt heavy as the lift shot upward.

"So, do you *lie* to everybody you first meet?" she yelled at Rex's holograph as it materialized next to them.

The holograph shrugged. "What's it say in that book of yours? 'Judge not lest ye be judged'?"

The elevator stopped and the door opened, revealing the video-illuminated corridor and a distant rectangle of blue-white daylight at the far end. Patrick followed right behind Oma, but before he could get off, the elevator doors slammed closed on Patrick's forward-stepping leg—right below the knee—really, really hard.

"Aahh!" he yelled, startled as much as he was in pain.

"Oh no! Patrick!" yelled Oma from outside the elevator. The doors were open just as wide as Patrick's shin bone, plus a bit of pinched flesh.

243

"One foot in this world, one in that," said Rex. "Isn't that always the way it is with transubstantiators like ourselves?"

"What should I do!?" yelled Oma, tugging at the doors along with Patrick, trying to force them open. They might as well have been trying to peel apart the bars of a prison window.

"Was I lying?" asked Rex, smiling not at all gently. "About the elevator having problems?"

"Run, Oma, run!" yelled Patrick.

"I'm not leaving you!" replied Oma. "We'll get you out!"

"How?" replied Patrick. His panic subsided as the logic of the situation solidified in his head. "You can't help me here. You can only help if you go get the others, if you get away. You can only help if he doesn't manage to close and lock the bunker door, too. *Run!*"

"Yes," said Rex's holograph. Its eyes rolled back and its face went slack, suddenly, as the real Rex, wherever he was, had his brain tap into the administrative data feed.

Oma paused a moment. "Should I take off your shoe so that you can at least get your leg back? Maybe you could pull it back through?"

"Run!" Patrick repeated. "You know he's not going to let me free! You know he'll catch you, too, if he can!"

Oma nodded and gave his toe-shoe a squeeze.

"I'll come back for you," she said.

"Maybe you won't have to," said Rex's holograph, smiling at Patrick in the elevator, his eyes focused once again.

"Run, Oma! Run!" Patrick yelled, looking out the elevator crack as her sprinting silhouette grew smaller and smaller against the distant daylight.

"Can you . . . side?" a voice crackled in his earpiece.

"Ivan!" yelled Patrick. "It's Rex!"

"I know . . . coming," came Ivan's staticky, staggered reply.

"Who's that?" said Rex. "Maybe the Anarchist tech expert who's been making so many problems for my Ith friends? So many fishies in this one little net!"

"Run!" Patrick screamed through the elevator gap. "Run, Oma, *run*!"

She looked to be almost to the doorway when there was a great flash, and her little figure fell to the ground.

"Oh!" said Patrick.

"Would you care to see what's going on up close?" asked Rex.

Patrick turned and saw Rex's holograph gesturing at the elevator's video walls. They were displaying the scene unfolding at the mouth of the bunker. Oma was lying on the concrete path just outside, completely still. Four storm-gray military sky-cars had settled in the clearing beyond the hill, and about twenty uniformed, gun-carrying commandos were emerging from their hinged cargo compartments.

The point of view shifted suddenly, and the big fir trees in which Ivan was hiding began to glow red.

"This is called Augmented Reality," observed Rex. "This is what my soldiers can see. This is how my soldiers are seeing where your hacker friend is, thanks to his transmissions."

"What's . . .'pening . . . two?" came Ivan's voice.

"Ivan, they're coming for you!" shouted Patrick.

"What . . . Oma?" came Ivan's voice.

"She's hurt!" shouted Patrick. "And I'm trapped!"

And he was. He pushed with all his might at the doors, pushed so that his chest and arms felt like they might break, pushed till his vision began to turn white. Pushed so hard he almost couldn't tell that the heavy metal doors hadn't budged a millimeter.

But even in his panic and stress and shame, he knew it was hopeless.

For the first time in days, he found himself wishing it was really all just a big fat dream.

CHAPTER 53

Prelude to Another Vanishing

MARY, RICK, LUCIE, EVA, AND CARLY EXITED THE park just below Seventy-Second Street, clambering over the low brown stone wall onto the sidewalk.

Mary wanted to text Nana to tell her to meet them back at the museum shortly, but she still had no service.

"Do you guys have any signal?" she asked.

Her three daughters and husband all looked at their phones and shook their heads.

"No bars at all," said Eva.

"In Midtown freaking Manhattan," said Rick. "So, if we didn't believe in Andrew's conspiracy theory already . . ."

"I think," replied Mary, "I lost any doubt after seeing that enormous rabbit get shot from a black helicopter and dragged into a van."

Carly asked suddenly, "Is he going to be okay?" and began crying.

"BunBun?" asked Lucie. "I think it was only a tranquilizer dart. They obviously could have killed him and didn't, right, Dad?"

"I think that's fair to say."

"But," said Eva, not crying herself but looking rather concerned. "What if they're going to torture him or something?"

"This isn't just weird," said Lucie. "This is seriously screwed up."

"Amen to that," said Mary, hugging her two younger daughters. "Come on, let's be strong and go find Nana and the Twins."

"And the freaky old dude from next door," said Lucie.

"Lucie," chided Rick, though he didn't do a very good job hiding his smile, "be respectful."

"There they are!" said Lucie. Coming down the sidewalk on the opposite side of the street were the distinctive shapes of their four-year-old siblings, their strangely graceful grandmother, and the gangly, lurching form of their odd next-door neighbor, Mr. Coffin.

The five Griffins crossed to the other side of the avenue and hurried toward them.

"Where's Deer Rabbit!?" shouted little Paul, running down the sidewalk with Cassie toward his family.

"Oh," said Mary, not knowing what to say.

"We couldn't get to him," said Rick, truthfully.

"Aw!" said both Twins.

"Did you understand what I meant when I said *special friend* in my text?" said Nana. "I didn't want to type out 'Bun-Bun' on account of the surveillance."

"You sent a text," said Mary.

"Telling us you were leaving the museum, I'm guessing," said Rick.

"It didn't go through?" said Nana.

"I'm sure it did," said Mary, showing her screen. "It's just that we have no signal."

"None of us," said Lucie, holding up her screen, too.

"But I still have signal," said Nana. "And, look, it says the text went through."

"And you have Ting, too, don't you?" said Rick.

"Ting?" asked Nana.

"The carrier, your cell-phone provider—remember, I helped you sign up for it last year?"

"Yes, yes, of course," said Nana, offering him her phone to look at. "I haven't changed a thing since then."

"So if it's not a company issue," said Rick, scrolling through her phone's settings, "and, look, you're CDMA just like all of ours—then the only explanation is that somebody has reached into the system and pinpointed us."

"What do you mean, Dad?" asked Eva.

"I mean, somebody must have intentionally found our phones on the system and taken them off the network."

"But doesn't that mean that somebody must be paying very close attention to us?" asked Mary.

As if to emphasize the point, a black van, blue strobes flashing, came speeding out of the park's Seventy-Second Street entrance and came to a screeching stop right in front of them.

CHAPTER 54
Foreign Language Instruction

THERE EEZ A COMPELLING NEATNESS," SAID THE little woman at the front of the church. "A profound and bee-oo-tee-ful ordair, to zee detailz of zees world zat constantly zreatens to seduce us from ow-air paths."

"What's she saying?" Neil asked. The woman's French accent, as she addressed the standing-room-only crowd, was pretty thick.

"Something philosophical, it sounds like," said Uncle Andrew. "Something about how false neatness and order can distract you from what you need to do."

"We must be strong," continued the little woman. "We must

not geeve een to zee selfeesh rules of bad govairnments and corporations!"

"Wild," said Dave.

"For my money, she makes a heck of a lot more sense than any of those white-toothed megachurch preachers," said Officer Murphy.

"What color are her teeth?" asked Neil.

Officer Murphy looked not quite down at Neil—she was only maybe an inch taller—but he definitely felt like a child as she replied, "There's not a thing wrong with her teeth or anything else about her. She's as she is meant to be."

"Hey, Hector," she said to the slender policeman standing at the last row of pews. "How's it going?"

"Good, Murph," replied the policeman. "Father Otis up there is keeping on top of things. She's going to do one-on-ones next."

Neil looked to the head of the line of people that extended up the right side of the church and saw a small man wearing one of those white-collared black priest shirts. He didn't look terribly on top of things to Neil. His eyes were closed and he was smiling like he was on drugs or something.

"And now, I weell read a pahssahj from zee book of Exodus," said the woman, opening a Bible to a page she'd marked with a ribbon marker. And here Neil had no trouble understanding what she said because, although her accent didn't lessen any, he'd heard the passage a bunch of times in church and church school. " 'And God said to Moses, I AM ZAT I AM: and he said, Zus shall you say to zee children of Israel, I AM has sent me to you.'

"Zat," she continued, her voice entirely big and bold like Queen Latifah's despite she herself not being any bigger than Neil's little brother, "is the entire pwont! Zee prophets, zay tell us that ALL ARE! I am. You are. We ALL ARE part of zee higher BE-ING. What I saw, what I was told on my journey, zees is TRUTH!"

The people in the church were clearly even more impressed. A collective murmur of awe went up and a couple people even staggered as she spoke.

"Now," she said in a smaller voice, "I weell continue to speak to you one by one, eef you like."

Neil hadn't noticed, but Officer Murphy had gone forward and spoken to the priest, who now in turn spoke to the woman. She had taken a glass of water from the pulpit and was just about to sit on the dais stair to speak to the people at the head of the line. She said something back to the priest, shot back up to her feet, and looked to the back of the church.

"Greeffins! There are some membairs of zee Greeffin family here!?"

Neil raised his hand, and the woman said loudly to the crowd, "I know many of you have been waiting to speak to me, and I will speak with you, but I first must see zeese people. I know sometheeng important zat I have to tell zem, a zeeng of great importance for zee world."

One or two people in the line might have looked a degree impatient as Officer Murphy waved Uncle Andrew and Neil forward, but mostly people seemed curious and maybe even a bit impressed that she was interested in them.

"Please, sit." She gestured to Neil and Uncle Andrew as

they came up to the dais. She resumed her seat on the stair as well.

"So," she said to Neil, "you are bigger zan me so I assume you are Patrick's beegger brozair."

"Yes," said Neil.

"You've met him?" asked Uncle Andrew.

"No, but on my very strange, very brief, journey, I 'eard from a friend of heez, a lovely friend. A greeeffin of anozair sort."

CHAPTER 55

Asunder

SOLDIERS WITH FLANGED RIOT HELMETS SPILLED
out of the van in front of the Griffins. They were wearing
black goggles pulled down over black ski masks, and they were
not messing around.

"You are Patrick Griffin's family, correct?" said the one
with three stripes on his shoulder.

"What do you know about Patrick!?" said Mary.

"We need your help to get him back," said the man. "Please
get into the van."

"What!?" said Rick. "Who are you people?"

"We are with the government," said the man. "There's no

time to discuss this now. Please, Mrs. Griffin, for the good of your son, we need you."

"Rick?" said Mary. "What do—"

"Don't trust them, Mom!" yelled Lucie. "Why would they need you to get—"

"Please get into the van," the man said to Mary.

"Or what?" said Rick.

Three soldiers emerged from the shadows, pistol-like weapons in their hands.

"You've got to be kidding me," said Rick, stepping in front of his wife. "Everybody, film this!" he yelled.

Nana and the rest of them raised their phones to take images but none of their screens—not even Nana's—came to life. They were completely dead. And meantime, the soldiers were clambering out of the van and moving toward them.

"We simply require your help over the next few days," said the man flatly, as if reading a script. "Please trust that this is the only way to ensure Patrick's safety. We must ask that you please speak to nobody about any of this. If you endeavor to draw any public attention to any of this, there will be repercussions, and the safety of other family members will be jeopardized."

"Are you threatening us?" asked Mary.

"You have till the count of five to get into the van," said the man with the stripes.

"You have till the count of three to apologize to my wife," Rick bellowed.

Over to the side, Mr. Coffin fumbled in the pockets of his tweed jacket.

"Five Missouri," said the man.

Rick stepped forward, his right hand balled into a fist.

"Four Missouri," said the man.

"You touch my wife, you touch any of us—" said Rick.

"Three Missouri," said the man.

Mr. Coffin sidled closer to the scene, his hand, no longer fidgeting, thrust in his pocket.

"Two Missouri," said the man.

Rick Griffin stepped forward, leaning into the goggled face of the man with the stripes.

"Rick!" shouted Mary.

"Dad!" shouted his eldest three daughters.

"Tell me where my son is!" shouted Rick into the man's face.

"One Missouri," replied the man, and dropped his hand.

In that moment three things happened in quick succession.

The soldier drew his weapon and shot Rick Griffin with a pair of tiny high-voltage electrodes, causing his body to jolt once and slump to the ground.

The three other soldiers stormed forward, grabbed Mary, and dragged her screaming to the van.

Mr. Coffin shouted "YAARG!" and, brandishing his can of self-defense spray, proceeded to stumble their way.

Unfortunately, the can didn't discharge and he found himself at the van door looking into the masked faces of the soldiers.

The man with the stripes addressed him and the still-conscious Griffins behind him.

"If you go to the authorities or draw any attention to this matter, we will kill her. And Patrick."

"Jesus wept!" the old man yelled as the door slid shut and he looked down at the can to see why it hadn't worked. He fumbled with the nozzle and, in a moment, determined that he simply hadn't pressed down hard enough on the release. As the van peeled away from the curb, a stream of pepper spray issued from the can, arcing up across his left cheek, eye, and forehead.

The scream he made was so high and loud that the variously wailing, shrieking, and paralyzed members of the Griffin family were momentarily distracted from their grief and shock.

Among them, only Nana had kept her head somewhat clear. She knelt down to ensure that Rick was merely unconscious, not dead. Then she gathered the wailing Twins in her arms and turned to the others.

"Lucie, Eva, Carly, let's get your father onto the sidewalk, then we'll deal with old Ichabod. It's just pepper spray. He'll be okay."

Throughout all of this, Lucie was struck by the fact that although there were people at either end of the sidewalk—a man in a cap, scarf, and cashmere coat looking like some old-fashioned movie director; a middle-aged woman with two teacup poodles; a young man slouching in a flannel shirt and skinny jeans—nobody had approached to offer help.

But now a young doorman had emerged from the apartment building behind them.

"Whoa!" he said, looking down at Rick, who was starting to stir. The doorman's accent sounded Jamaican. "Is the man all right? Is there anything I can do? I called nine-one-one a'ready."

Nana turned to him.

"Thank you for being so kind," she said. Rick was muttering something. "What we really need are a couple of taxis."

The man leapt out into the street and, in less than two minutes, had flagged as many down.

CHAPTER 56
Bunker Hill Massacre

PATRICK LOOKED ON IN HORROR AT THE SPLIT-screen elevator display.

The left side showed six soldiers moving toward the bunker; the right side showed the twenty-plus commandos moving toward the trees.

"This situation . . . very . . . up," came Ivan's voice.

"Ivan, I'm so sorry," said Patrick. "We should have known—we should—"

"Not . . . blame . . . me," the man replied.

"That's so sweet," said Rex's holograph. "Look how honorable you are being. You know, you do—despite the odds—have a spark of leadership in you, young man."

Patrick briefly made eye contact with the holograph and then looked back at the screen showing the soldiers approaching Oma's sprawled body.

"Let me ask," continued Rex. "What is it that has driven you into the arms of these fools? What was it that made you decide that I am the bad guy here?"

"Let my friends go, and maybe I'll talk to you," said Patrick.

"Ha!" laughed the holograph. "That's what I'm talking about. That's *exactly* what I look for when I hire somebody. That problem-solving spark, that testing of the levers even when the person is unsure if what he's touching is a lever or an immovable piece of structural steel."

The soldiers approaching Oma could see her body now, having stepped onto the pathway leading into the bunker's recessed entrance.

On the other screen, the soldiers had reached the trees and were cautiously converging on the spot.

Ivan began to haltingly sing,

"Mine eyes have . . . seen the . . . glory
of the . . . coming of . . . the word—"

"Poor Ivan," said Rex. "What's the old saying? 'He's got a face for radio and a voice for sword-swallowing.' Let's shut that off, shall we?"

The comm link in Patrick's hood crackled and fell silent.

"My boy," continued Rex's holograph. "I *do* hope I can get you to reconsider your role in all of this. It would be such a triumph for humanity if this random occurrence—this very strange confluence of events that has resulted in your transubstantiation to Ith—could be viewed by the people of Ith as a seamless chapter in our story. Think about it. What if you were to be the next *me*? My protégé, my deputy, my *guy*."

"So I could help enslave people, and spy on them, and kill *billions*?"

"Oh dear," replied Rex, shaking his holographic head. "What have people been telling you? How those silly Commonplacers distort the simplest things! My boy, if only you could have seen what I saw through my eyes today! The wondrous achievements of your Ith brethren, the miraculous order and harmony that has been forged here on this world. These have never before been even approximated in all of human history, on *either* of the worlds!"

Patrick had an instinct to ask Rex why he said "either of the worlds"—was he intentionally leaving out Mindth?—but just then the soldiers in the display reached down and grabbed Oma's body and turned her over. One of them began to run medical sensors up and down the length of her body, and then another one kicked her in the ribs.

"Tell them to stop! Don't hurt her!" he shouted.

"Ah," said Rex. "Tell you what, you take off that silly hood, and I'll see what I can do. I like to see the faces of the people I'm speaking with."

Patrick immediately pulled down his suit's headpiece. There was no point to it anymore now that the comm link had been severed.

"Much better," said Rex. "You look much less like a criminal now."

"Don't let them hurt her!" yelled Patrick.

Rex laughed like somebody had told a funny story at a church coffee hour. "And how about your other friend?" he asked Patrick.

From the helmet-cam of a soldier, the wall display was now showing Ivan clapping on the ground by the tree where Patrick and Oma had left him. He was still singing his song, and smiling, right up to when another soldier kicked him in the ribs. Another came up and pulled the foil off his collar's receiver. Ivan's body immediately stood, bowed dramatically—like a Russian prince—and then got down on the ground and crawled to one soldier's boots, where he pressed his wincing head into them, as if to deliver a kiss. Then he crawled to another and did the same.

The soldiers thought this was hilarious. Patrick figured out that one of them was operating Ivan's collar-control through his binky.

"You never really expected me to voluntarily join you, did you?" said Patrick, his stomach in knots.

"Why do you say that?" asked Rex.

"Because why would you show me this!? You don't humiliate the friends of a person you're trying to impress. What do you really want!?"

"Outstanding!" said Rex. "Dispassionate analytic thinking under duress! Do you know that less than one in one hundred thousand kids your age questions motives in adversarial scenarios like this? I swear I don't believe in conspiracy but, every once in a while, one does feel a certain justifiable degree of paranoia. The first accidental Earth-Ith transub in more than a century is a kid who is at the top of the charts with his situational social IQ? What are the odds?!"

He smiled a smile that made the skin on the back of Patrick's neck tingle.

"I asked you a question," said Rex. "What are the odds?"

"What? How would I know?"

"You know of no conspiracy involving your arrival on Ith the first time? Nobody contacted you before your transubstantiation? Did you have any visions or dreams that you might consider to be premonitions, perhaps?"

"What? No. I had no idea Ith even existed—" Patrick broke off and sucked breath. The elevator doors were pressing harder upon his leg. Bolts of pain traveled up and down his shinbone. He wondered if it might give way, suddenly collapse, cracking like a walnut in a pair of pliers.

"You seem to have gone a bit pale," said Rex. "Everything okay?"

"The doors," gasped Patrick. He was gripping the doors with both hands, vainly trying to relieve the pressure. He could feel the motors straining harder and harder to clamp all the way shut.

"That's so terrible," said Rex. "The doors have your lower leg, is it? Your tibia?"

"What?" asked Patrick.

"Your tibia. That's the bigger bone in your lower leg—the shinbone. The one behind is called the fibula, the calf-bone."

Patrick rocked forward and grabbed the collar of his skinsuit in his mouth so he could bite down on it.

"I'd like to help, but you see, somebody hacked the system,

and it's causing all kinds of issues. Now, if you were able to tell me something to put my mind a little at ease here, it might help me remember how to engage the emergency override protocols. The sequence is really at the tip of my tongue and, if I could just have a reason to calm down and think clearly . . . I am so terribly distracted, you see, trying to find that misdirected griffin and his vandalistic henchmen. Maybe if you could help me locate them, some weight would shift from my mind and I would be able to recall how to turn off the power to that silly malfunctioning elevator."

Patrick bit down harder to keep himself from talking, but in a moment he wondered if he'd be able to form words if he tried. He had never felt anything like this in his entire life. His arms strained, his other leg pushed against the doors, his back arched, and his jaw clenched down on the collar of his shirt as he tried to stifle the scream that was building in his chest.

He looked to Rex's holograph at one point, hoping to see some sort of indication, some sort of hopeful anything that he was going to stop the doors from squeezing. But the horrible man was just standing there with a mildly expectant look on his humorless, cleft-chinned face.

Patrick's mind bounced like a marble in a three-color roulette wheel: he could beg, he could scream, or he could continue to fight the pain. They were the only choices he could conceive. The first two were dark and unappealing, but the third was becoming harder and harder to envision.

What was this? This was not a pain like when he'd fallen off the slide as a little kid and gotten three stitches; this was not like when he'd gone to the hospital with his shellfish allergy and his whole head had swelled up like a balloon and he'd barely been able to breathe.

And it wasn't just the pain radiating up his leg and somehow into the center of his brain. This was not just the white-hot, searing sensation that a huge barbecue skewer had been thrust up from his calf right out the top of his head, and was slowly twisting.

This was also the sensation of being entirely alone. There was no Mom. There was no Dad. There was nothing but the pain.

The doors were grinding closer and closer together, and now it occurred to him they might actually snip his leg clean off like a big dull pair of scissors.

And then there was a burning sensation on his right forearm.

He looked down at his arms, both still vainly straining against the mechanical might of the doors. The sleeve of his skin-suit had ridden up his forearm and he could see that the letters of the scar—the scar from the hot pipe under the kitchen sink, right before he'd transubstantiated to Ith the first time—were *glowing* white, glowing like his arm was filled with electricity.

The scar, which was essentially a reverse brand of some of the letters on the drain pipe he'd bumped against, read *YA-WAY*.

Was the pain making him hallucinate? What was happening? Was he being electrocuted on top of everything else?

The pain of his leg had entirely gone away now, but he could see and sense the doors continuing to crush closer and closer, and then there was the most amazing voice in his head, his mother's voice.

It said simply, "I am."

"I am?" Patrick said aloud.

"Yes," said the voice calmly. "You are."

Patrick felt like laughing somehow. The gap between the elevator doors was no wider than his thumb now. How could his leg even fit inside a gap that small? He looked at his straining fingers, past the brightly glowing scar of his forearm.

YA-WAY.

"So weird," he muttered to himself and then, deciding there was no point losing the tips of his fingers, too, he jerked his hands from the gap.

And then Patrick heard—fortunately more than he felt—first his tibia, then his fibula shatter as the elevator doors finally found each other.

He passed out a moment later.

CHAPTER 57
Birthdaygram

MARY GRIFFIN DIDN'T KNOW WHAT TO THINK. AND that was okay because her unfettered emotions were occupying every lobe, fiber, and fissure of her mind. Principally, these feelings were:

Surprise at having been abducted in broad daylight, thrown in a van, and driven more than an hour without any sign from her captors that they were even worried about being caught.

Revulsion at these mask-wearing soldiers, dressed all in black and not betraying a flicker of humanity. Taping her wrists and ankles, making her swallow some sort of pill—they said it would cause her no harm—and then gagging her and putting a hood over her head.

Fear at the threats made by the man with some European accent—German, French, Dutch, she didn't know. They had Patrick. And Patrick would suffer, Patrick would *die* if she didn't do exactly what they said.

Confusion at the nature of the instructions she was given as they laid her on her back in the narrow little room. And then them asking her to think of her favorite poem, song, or expression. *Mantra* was the word they had used. (They had kidnapped her, placed her in this tiny room, and now expected her to *meditate?*)

Resignation at knowing that however insane this all seemed, there was absolutely nothing she could do about it, not if she believed them about having Patrick's fate in their hands. And why wouldn't she believe them? If they could helicopter sniper teams into Central Park in broad daylight, shoot a giant jackalope, and then steal a mother of seven from an Upper West Side sidewalk, clearly they were at least capable of abducting a twelve-year-old boy. What choice did she have but to play along?

So she relaxed like they said. And she had absolutely no trouble coming up with a song to sing herself.

It worked remarkably well. Even as she smelled the church incense, coughed once, twice, three times, the words were there, guiding her fleeing thoughts as surely as a canyon conducts a river.

Even through her blindfold everything went fluorescently

white. And then the richest, deepest, most vernal green she'd ever experienced. And she kept on singing even when she knew it was all done, and that she was no longer in the little room:

"Happy birthday to you,
Happy birthday to you,
Happy birthday, dear Patrick . . ."

CHAPTER 58
Alive & Alone

THREE OF THE NINE—BARB, TRIXY, AND SHORTY— found each other under the next highway bridge. There was no sign of the others. They waited nearly an hour, knowing better than to be out in the open, but periodically peering around the bridge's buttresses when there was no sign of any boats on the river, or people on the shore. And also, of course, when they weren't crying too hard to see.

Even Barb was broken up. Two thirds of her family was missing, missing under circumstances that had involved silenced but still-quite-deadly bullets raining down into the water as they'd swum away from the boat. Barb and Trixy and Shorty had heard them ripping through the water all around them.

Perhaps the others hadn't just heard, but felt them. Perhaps their bodies were drifting out toward the ocean even as they huddled here, cowardly, cold, but unable to conceive of anything else they *could* do.

They had known the risks. They had known what had to be done. They had sent nine—plus BunBun—knowing that just one of them had to make it through, just one of them needed to raise the alarm, and needed to deliver the speech, to prevent the end of this world as everybody knew it.

And what would then happen to the other worlds.

"We have to get moving," said Trixy, touching Barb and Shorty on their striped backs.

They knew it was so, and followed her up under the bridge to an embankment, and into the city that was the capital of the mightiest nation on Earth.

CHAPTER 59
Operation Camel Drop

IT WAS JUST AS WELL THE BOY HAD PASSED OUT. There would be time to work on him later. And it wasn't like he would be going anywhere.

Rex regarded the feed from the bunker elevator one last time—the crumpled body on the floor, its left foot and lower leg extending out of sight—and reduced the pressure on the doors holding the crushed leg. There was no sense cutting off the blood flow entirely. If the boy was cooperative in coming days, he might even instruct the medical team to repair the thing. And—he smiled at the thought—if the boy was especially useful, he might even let the medical team use anesthetics during the procedure.

But all those considerations could wait. Rex, who had been standing in the screen-lit room of his Pacific seaside residential compound, now turned his attention to the situation unfolding outside the Northifornian bunker. Somehow a single enemy flier had appeared in the sky above the location where the teams had been capturing the boy, the girl, and the old programmer.

He immediately scrambled fighters to intercept it, but they were still terts away. In the meantime, a lone creature—one he recognized almost immediately as being the leader of his enemies, the griffin named My-Chale—dropped something.

Rex immediately suspected a bomb, but of course that didn't make any sense. A bomb could harm the boy, the girl, friend Ivan—and his cameras shortly showed it wasn't a bomb but a creature, one that at least very much resembled a camel.

"Is he insane?" Rex wondered aloud, and not just because dropping a single one of his Mindthling friends into a platoon of heavily armed soldiers was probably not going to accomplish much. Flying in daylight like this meant that even with his fighter jets minutes away, drones and satellites would be able to track My-Chale wherever he went. There could be no escape for him this time.

"Track the griffin and capture it alive!" he shouted. His feed was already displaying four different camera angles on the flying, lion-bodied enemy leader. And a real-time three-dimensional map showed the creature's progress and exact location as it flew toward the eastern mountains.

Rex shifted his attention to the five camera streams that featured the dropped camel. The falling creature appeared to be conscious but entirely unpanicked as it plunged to the ground, its body slowly rotating. Its gangly legs and long neck lolled on the cushion of rushing air. It was wearing a backpack of sorts, crushed down on its back. The purpose of the pack was soon clear: it contained a large white parachute, which deployed approximately five hundred meters from the ground. In addition to slowing the camel's descent to a survivable speed, it revealed a message.

Black letters had been stitched across the canopy that read,

meek will inherit
Rex will suck it

Rex blanched and ordered his soldiers on the ground to hold their fire and capture the creature alive for interrogation. It appeared to be entirely unarmed.

The camel landed and fell on its side.

"Help me get this silly parachute off, will you?" she said to the soldiers who surrounded her.

The squad leader heard Rex's commands (given via the standard YSS command chain, as Rex was still keeping his presence on Ith a secret) and silently signaled for two soldiers to remove the harness from the camel's back.

"You are under arrest," announced the squad leader.

"Ah, well," said the camel. "Can't win 'em all."

Rex noted that the camel seemed normal in every way other than having red hair and a misshapen hump. It was a strange thing that rose like a fur-covered, flat-topped flowerpot from the center of its back.

He instructed the YSS Deacons to retrieve the boy from the bunker elevator and ensure he was medically stable. A transport would soon be arriving to take him and the other prisoners—camel included—to Silicon City.

The boy was still unconscious, the girl was not talking, and the programmer was still trying to sing, but the camel was talking up a storm.

Rex turned his attention back to the feed from the soldiers surrounding it.

"Please," said the camel. "Just a little?"

"You can have water later," said the commanding officer.

"But I'm so thirsty," said the camel. "Please?"

"You're a camel, take it easy," said the officer. His soldiers laughed.

"Actually, I'm an EMP camel," said the camel.

"All right, I'll ask," said the officer. "What's an *emp* camel?"

"A camel with the ability to make an EMP, of course," said the camel.

"An emp?"

"Yes but only every once in a while. It's terribly taxing."

"Taxing?" said the officer.

"Hard to do," said the camel. "Witness—" she started to say and proceeded to scrunch up her face, contract her neck, bend her knees, and generally look as if she were going to cough up a hairball, or do something even grosser from the other end. And then the hump on her back began to glow.

"Kill it! Kill it quickly!" screamed Rex.

But it was too late. There was a brilliant flash, and every piece of electrical equipment in a thirty-kilometer radius was immediately disabled. Nearby drones and the fighters chasing My-Chale fell from the sky, the cameras in the soldiers' suits stopped working, as did their weapons and binkies, and, inside the bunker, everything went dark.

Emp, Rex had just realized, stood for electromagnetic pulse—the phenomenon that occurs when a nuclear weapon is discharged and causes a blast of electromagnetic radiation that will overwhelm conventional circuitry.

Inside his beachfront compound, Rex groaned in frustration as his theater feeds went black.

CHAPTER 60

Little Drummer Boy

WHAT DO YOU MEAN, 'A GRIFFIN OF ANOTHER sort'?" Uncle Andrew asked the old French woman, Lilian Carruth.

"I mean like a lion with wings, and zee 'ead of a beautiful eagle," she replied. "I was standing zare een zees field and ee came to me as eef in a vision, a dream."

"Like a *griffin* griffin," said Neil. "Like what Lucie dreamed of the other night."

Uncle Andrew nodded, and not just to be polite. It was crazy—he was a man of science, a chemist, a disciple of logic and rationality. And yet he believed this woman. Lucie had dreamed of a griffin. And his other nieces' and nephews' encounter with a giant talking jackalope. There was no reason for any of them to lie, for one thing.

"It was such a short time, but I learned so much from him—'is name was My-Chale. He warned me," she continued in her thick accent, which Neil felt he was getting better at interpreting, "not to speak of it publicly—the bad ones, the ones in the smartphones and in the computers—they are hearing my words and they may grow impatient if I say something that will make it seem like I am not just a religious nutjob, a weirdo. But he—his name was My-Chale—he hoped the boy, the Patrick Griffin boy, that his family would find me. That we could talk. Are you his father?" she said, turning to Uncle Andrew.

"I'm his uncle," he said, "his mother's brother."

"Ah, his uncle," she said, "and I can tell you and he are close. He has a very important job that has fallen to him. He is a brave boy, yes?"

"A very brave boy," said Uncle Andrew. "Very good at keeping his mind even when the world around is not as one might want it."

"You agree about your brotherr?" she said to Neil.

Neil shrugged agreeably. "Yeah, Patrick marches to his own drum, that's for sure."

The woman laughed and pantomimed a little drumroll. "Well, on my strange little journey, My-Chale, he told me that he is a very good little drummer boy. You should be very proud to be a part of his life."

"Drummer boy?" asked Andrew.

"Yes, drummer boy," said the woman.

"And he's okay?"

"He's safe, I hear, and he is aware."

"Aware?"

"He knows that he IS, he knows that he is NOT DREAM-ING, he knows that what he does matters. Matters very much. Which is not as common a thing as we might like to think."

Uncle Andrew nodded, although his head was swirling with a million unanswered questions. The two at the head of the churning parade were, "Where is this griffin? Where is Patrick?"

"They are both in the other place," said the woman. "The place called Ith. The same place where the bad man was, and where he has gone again."

"Bad man?" asked Neil.

"Rex Abraham," said the old woman. "You have heard of him?"

"Yes," said Andrew. "We have heard of him."

"Yes, he is very bad. He embraces Death because he can be confined and controlled, whereas Life . . . she will never sit still for her portrait."

"What do you mean?"

"Shh," she said, nodding at a man entering the church and putting up a fuss about having to give up his cell phone. "We must not say his name again. They are listening. I can talk of crazy speaking monsters and your boy on a world where people have big eyes and small ears. They will say I'm a lunatic and that is what people will believe. But we must not again speak this name I have said. That is where they worry, still worry, even though there are only days left for us to do anything about it, about him.

280

"Go now, know Patrick is alive, and come back and see me tomorrow at five o'clock. We have one thing we can do, and we must do it together. You are staying here in this town? In Corpus Christi?"

"Yes, a hotel just a few blocks away."

"Good." She looked up at the priest and said loudly, "Father Otis, please get the Griffins' hotel information. I need to start talking to these other people." She gestured at the line of hopeful people behind Andrew and Neil.

They left the church, stepping out into the warm Gulf of Mexico night.

"You boys seem happier than when you went in—what'd you find out?" asked Dave.

"I don't know what we found out, Dave," said Uncle Andrew, "but I'm glad we came. I think we at least got ourselves some hope."

"Well, I'm glad for that," said the big man.

"You're feeling better, too, Neil?"

"Yeah," said Neil. "I think we at least have a sign that Patrick's okay."

"Good, good!" said Dave.

"Say," said Neil. "Do you know how far the aquarium is?"

"The Texas State Aquarium? Oh, a ten-minute drive from here depending on traffic. Why?"

"I was thinking, since we have to wait around until tomorrow, maybe we can go see that squid they caught."

"Sure," said Andrew. "A giant squid. Why not?"

CHAPTER 61

Healing Hands

PATRICK WOKE WITH A START, AND IMMEDIATELY wished he'd done so with a pause instead—the sudden movement had caused his left leg to shift, and his left leg, or what was left of it, didn't appreciate it.

The pain that had made him pass out in the first place came flooding back. No longer biting down on the fabric of his skin-suit, he screamed with all his might, only letting off a little when he sensed his hand being squeezed.

He opened his eyes and saw a yellow-green light all around him. He wanted to scream again but he'd entirely run out of breath.

"It's okay, Patrick," said a voice—Oma's voice.

"Keep him still if you can," said another voice. A voice he recognized. "It's the nerves reconnecting." The yellow-green light, a swarm of fireflies, suddenly made sense.

"Laurence?" Patrick said, sucking breath and looking around again.

"Yes, here," said Laurence's voice. "Here, breathe deep. This should help the pain."

Patrick inhaled as Laurence pressed something cool and plastic against his nose and mouth.

Oma was looking at him with concern.

"You've been asleep a long time," she said.

"Shock will do that to a person," said Laurence's voice.

"Are we in your cave?" asked Patrick, trying to see past the will-o'-the-wisp's glow. He couldn't tell what Laurence had done, but the pain was indeed going away and his senses seemed to be coming back. Still, everything past the partly illuminated shape of Oma's head was dark.

"Not the same cave as last time," she replied. "We took advantage of Edna's flash to find a new hideout."

"Edna's flash?"

"Yes, Edna the EMP camel. She'd never done it before but we'd all seen it in the dream when she arrived from Mindth. She seems like a regular talking camel except her hump contains a unique organ that can create a massive electromagnetic pulse. A pulse that can basically fry all electronic circuits for dozens of kilometers around. It'll take a few yies to grow back, but she should be okay.

"So, we took advantage of the hole it punched in the Deacons' surveillance network and relocated. That's how My-Chale and the others managed to come back and rescue us."

"That was pretty convenient," observed Patrick, clarity coming back to him in waves. "Having a friend who happens to have the ability to blow out the Deaconry's electronics."

"Yes," said Laurence. "Sometimes it almost seems as if Mindth has a purpose in sending us the people—or griffins, or EMP camels, or jackalopes, or boys—it sends us."

"What about Ivan?" asked Patrick. "Is he okay?"

"Fortunately—very fortunately—the pulse fried his collar's circuits, too. He knew the EMP was going to disable the collar, but whether harmlessly or by triggering its kill-switch we just didn't know. Of course there was no way to find out without trying. So, yes, he's fine and in fact has full control of his body again. As does every collar-camp intern that was within thirty clicks of the blast. We rescued nearly three hundred of them in total. Now we just need to figure out how to hide and feed them. Which is, as you might imagine, a logistical nightmare."

"Is Seth taking care of him?"

"They killed Seth," said My-Chale.

"What?" said Patrick.

"His spirit lives on," said Oma. "And his words are now part of the *Commonplace*."

Another jolt of pain racked Patrick's body just then—a bone-traveling shock wave that began with his leg and ended inside his skull—but he managed not to scream.

"Sorry, that should be the worst of it," said Laurence. "I gave you a pretty good breath of ether, but that leg is going to ache pretty fiercely from time to time. The doors didn't just snip it off—they *crushed* a good portion of your lower leg bones."

"My tibia and fibula," said Patrick.

"Precisely," said Laurence.

"So, you're adept with anatomy as well as chemistry," said a kindly voice.

"My-Chale!" said Oma.

"How was Rex, Patrick?"

"Umm, awful," said Patrick, shuddering at the memory of his time in the elevator with Rex's holograph.

Oma squeezed his hand.

"Yes, he generally is," replied My-Chale.

Patrick nodded and finally got the courage to look down at his left leg, expecting to find it ending in a bandaged stump where the elevator doors had cut it off. Instead, he saw his foot.

"You re-attached my leg?!" asked Patrick.

"You've got some traction and casts in your future—no kill the carrier for at least a month—but you ought to recover," said Laurence. "The others are fashioning you a nice brace and some crutches. You should be able to get around starting tomorrow."

"Laurence is good at what he does," said Oma.

"Also helps to have stolen some good nanosurgical grafting kits from the enemy," confessed Laurence.

"Thank you, Laurence," said Patrick.

"My pleasure," said Laurence. "How's the pain now?"

"Okay other than feeling like a failure," said Patrick.

"What do you mean by that?" asked My-Chale.

"I basically got stuck in an elevator. And I caused us to use up, umm, Edna's weapon. And, Seth . . ."

"Nobody sacrificed unwillingly," said My-Chale. "And nothing was done in vain. We discovered something very important."

"EMPs work really well against the Deacons?" asked Oma.

"They did this time," said My-Chale. "But the Deacons will adapt quickly, as they always do. No, what we discovered was that Mindth is very aware of *you*, Patrick."

"What does that mean?" Patrick asked.

"I think it means we need to send you to the slumbering world," said My-Chale.

"Mindth?" said Patrick.

"What?" said Oma. "Is that even possible?"

"We'll discuss later," said My-Chale.

"First," said Laurence, "our patient needs to do some slumbering himself."

Patrick nodded. He was pretty sure he wasn't dreaming this entire conversation, but it was entirely possible. What he did know was that whatever drug Laurence had given him was making him very sleepy, and that he could feel Oma's hand around his.

EPILOGUE

LET ME GO, PLEASE," SAID THE VOICE. "I'M DYING."
"Not yet, you're not," said John Simon. The ship had
just docked. The creature was being kept alive for Rex's return.

"You don't want this to happen," said the voice. "If it does,
if you do this to Earth, there will be no coming back."

John Simon was again struck by the beauty of the creature's
voice, but he knew better. Although she might sound like a
sweet, sympathetic, lost kid, she was 100 percent monster. A
fifteen-foot-long telepathic squid that could talk inside nearby
people's heads even through a ship's metal bulwark.

He smirked and hit the metal wall of the enormous tank
with the butt of his weapon.

"Please," said the voice, and again he found himself dangerously inclined to her words. "Listen to your own reason. You know nothing good will come of a tragedy this enormous. Every human you are about to make suffer and die has every bit as much validity as you do. They are just as real as you are. What they see through their eyes, what they hear through their ears, what they feel—you *know* it's just as real as what you experience with your own senses. And their dreams—"

"Enough!" John Simon yelled at the metal wall. He'd been trained along with all his fellow aspirants to Earth's coming Deaconry.

"Don't make me turn on the lights again!" he said.

"Please," said the voice. Somehow the creature sounded close to tears despite the fact that it was impossible—or at least pointless—to cry underwater.

"Please, please don't—I'll stop talking."

"Yes, yes, you will. And if you try any tricks—"

"I won't," said the squid, though she didn't mean it, not really.

She didn't have a lot of tricks to play, but she did have one. At least until the Griffin boy's family got in touch.

As she was hoping they would.

As she'd dreamed they would.

THE TWELVE TENETS OF
Rex Abraham

1. Promote order.
2. Combat entropy.
3. Shun the sickness of uncertainty.
4. Resist the contagion of complacency.
5. Conserve resources.
6. Respect directives.
7. Achieve measurable productivity in all tasks.
8. Seek all actionable knowledge.
9. Provide all actionable knowledge to your admins.
10. Do not harm the flesh of any living creature.
11. Do not alter the flesh of any living creature.
12. Disobey the Minder's emissaries in nothing.

Don't miss Book 3 in the

PATRICK GRIFFIN

AND THE THREE WORLDS series!

· · · · ·

Coming Summer 2018